Imposter

Fletcher Felix

ISBN 979-8-9935409-1-7 (paperback)

Book Cover by Fletcher Felix

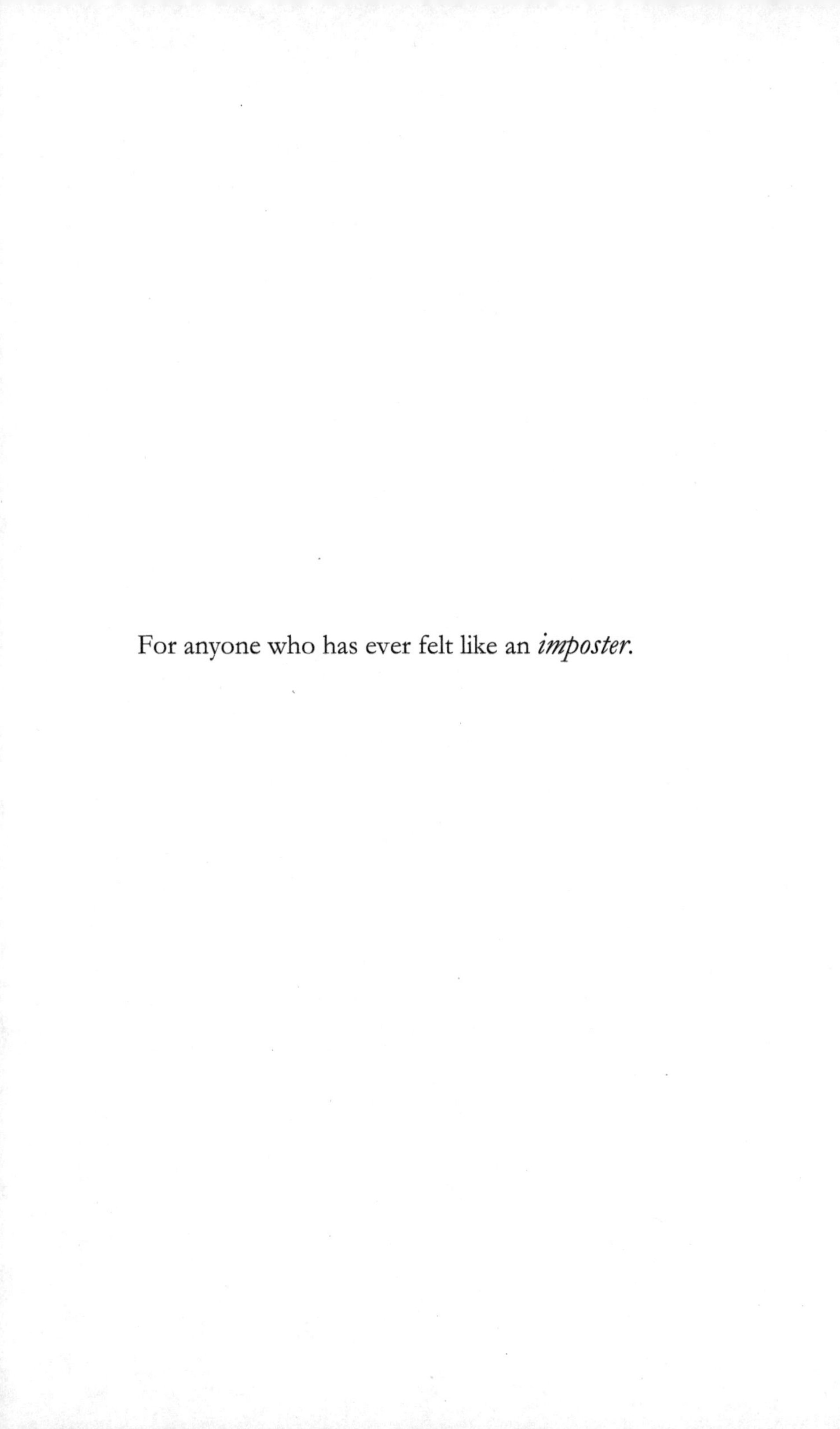

For anyone who has ever felt like an *imposter*.

Prologue

The guttural sound of my husband's snore wakes me from a fitful slumber.

As my eyelids peel open in the darkness of our bedroom, I feel the gnawing pain of my overused muscles immediately. Even my eyelids are tender. Hours of dragging and digging have taken their toll. I rub my sore forearms and roll onto my side slowly, bringing my husband's sleeping body into view.

He looks just as he always does. His dark wavy hair always slightly messy, his olive skin so effortlessly glowing and sun kissed. The gentle rise of his chest emitting small snorts and snores.

But that is not my husband.

My husband lies in an unmarked grave, the maggots and rot slowly devouring his lifeless body.

I killed my husband, only to wake up beside an imposter.

Chapter One

I sit in the fourth row of pews from the front. The same pew I sit in every Sunday since I was a little girl. My husband sits to my right, as he has done every Sunday for the last twelve years. The pastor drones on in his monotone voice, making it difficult to hold the attention of the congregation, and I glance at the side of my husband's face. What is he doing here? What is he doing still breathing air? I find myself feeling irrationally annoyed at this man for simply existing.

I know how this sounds…I don't hate the man, I really don't. I wouldn't say I love him either, but I must have at some point. Now, it's simply a neutral feeling. An I have accepted my fate, feeling. A feeling brought on by losing love long ago, but knowing that I can never divorce. Divorce would be looked down upon; I could be shunned by the very community that has meant everything to me. I simply cannot risk it. I have no choice, really.

"Are you okay?" My husband's whispered voice intrudes my thoughts.

"Yes, yes, of course." I whisper in return, turning my attention back to the pastor.

So, that is how we are going to play it. Pretend everything is fine. So predictable of our marriage.

I think back to last night's dinner of lasagna and garlic bread. Everything homemade, of course. Shortly after we married, it was decided that I would be a homemaker, and Billy would bring home the bacon. At first, I enjoyed spending my time baking, keeping a tidy home and hosting weekly gatherings for all our friends and neighbors.

But it got old quick.

Don't get me wrong, I am not unhappy in my life. It is all I have ever known. I am very active in my church, and have a number of friends and hobbies. I am not even unhappy in my marriage really, but I guess I am bored. And you know what they say about idle hands and the devil's workshop.

Before I could even serve the lasagna, the hemlock in Billy's diet coke did its job. At least, I thought it did. Was it nothing more than a dream my brain concocted while lying next to Billy's snoring body? It all felt so real.

No.

It *was* real.

There is no way possible it was a dream. I have been thinking about this for months. I painstakingly acquired the hemlock, choosing not to risk trying to grow it myself. It wasn't a dream.

If it really wasn't a dream, then why is my husband still sitting next to me?

After the service has finished, I head to the table in the back of the nave where many of the members are now congregating. I grab a Styrofoam cup, pouring coffee into it and stir in an absurd amount of sugar. I can practically hear my mother's voice ringing in my ear, her southern twang thick as molasses. *All that sugar makes perfect sense…you never were sweet enough on your own.*

“Hey Kiki!” a squeal of a voice emits from the crowd, a petite blond hurrying toward me.

“Good morning, Lucy.” I attempt to sound as interested as possible, but my mind is elsewhere.

“Are you still coming to the bake sale this Thursday?” She asks, her voice rising as the question comes to its end.

“Of course, I am. I’m making my famous snickerdoodles and a few gingerbread cakes.”

Lucy claps her hands together, an excited smile on her obviously spray tanned face. I squint my eyes a bit to avoid the aggressively white shade of her teeth burning my retinas.

“I love your snickerdoodles. I’m looking forward to it!” She squeals, her hands still clapping together like a small child.

“Yeah, me too.” I mutter.

I am, in fact, *not* looking forward to the bake sale this Thursday. The amount of snickerdoodle cookies and gingerbread cakes I have made for this church over the years could fill the entire building. That's what a good little housewife does. She bakes for the church. She loves her neighbors. *She doesn't kill her husband.* Maybe I'm not so perfect after all.

I sip the last of my coffee, looking at the dregs remaining in the bottom of the cup. It is unlike me to be so antisocial, quietly emptying my cup on the outskirts of the regular crowd. I am just not feeling it today. Like so many times in the last few years, I force myself to smile and pretend that everything is normal.

Everything is *perfect.*

Chapter Two

We return home after socializing for an hour and fall into our usual Sunday routine. Billy sits in front of the television, the noise of a football game blasting loudly from the speakers. I am in the kitchen washing the breakfast dishes I abandoned prior to leaving for church.

I replay last night in my head yet again, feeling the soreness in my arms as I recall dragging my husband's body in our dining room and rolling him onto the waiting sled. How could a dream have been so vivid? Every detail planned, every moment clearly remembered.

I am thrust back into reality as the sound of my husband's voice rises above the television.

"Can you grab me a beer, honey?"

"Of course!" I shout back automatically.

I dry my hands on the kitchen towel and reach into the refrigerator, wrapping my fingers around the neck of a cold beer bottle. I freeze; eyes locked on the Pyrex Tupperware container sitting on the top shelf. I run my fingers along the dark green top, thinking of the trees surrounding me as I dragged the sled that carried my husband's body through the woods behind our house. I grab the container filled with last night's leftovers and quickly lift the lid. A whole lasagna stares back at me, looking nearly as pristine as the moment I took it out of the oven. Not a single piece cut, not a single bite taken.

So, we didn't eat last night. I guess I didn't really have time to make myself a plate since I spent hours digging a husband sized hole. And Billy? Well, I guess you don't need dinner when you're dead.

A very much alive Billy shouts from the comfort of his favorite chair again. "You okay in there?"

Code for hurry up. I roll my eyes.

I quickly place the lasagna back on the shelf and grab a bottle of beer, shutting the refrigerator door with my hip.

I hand the bottle to Billy wordlessly and smile as if it was an absolute pleasure to drop what I am doing to cater to his needs.

"Thanks honey." He states, eyes glued on the screen in front of him.

I turn to leave the room and return to the dishes, nearly making it into the hallway before I speak again. "Oh, don't forget, we are having the Millers over for dinner tomorrow night."

A grunt.

I take that as a response and continue toward the waiting dishes.

Chapter Three

I wake the next morning to the sound of Billy's alarm, and again find myself disappointed to see that he is still breathing. At least we will be having Lucy and her husband over for dinner tonight, that will give me something different to put my efforts into today.

I rub the sleep from my eyes and gingerly touch the curlers wrapped in my auburn red hair. Billy silently slides out of the comforter and slinks toward the bathroom. His arms hang heavy, feet dragging noisily. He must have slept terribly, as he is typically a morning person. I have never enjoyed early mornings, so I usually find it quite annoying to have a husband that is practically ready to perform a musical before the sun has even woken up.

I sit up in bed and close my eyes, repeating a few positive affirmations in my head.

I have the power to change and grow.

I am peaceful and my life is infused with calm.

I learn from my mistakes and improve every day.

I open my eyes and sigh. I have never been good with this affirmation stuff, but Lucy swears by it. Maybe my next improvement should be getting better at murder.

My toes touch the hardwood floor and I cringe at the unwelcome cold against my skin. Padding to the bathroom, I peek in to see Billy putting his contact lenses into his eyes. As I reach the double sinks, I glance down and see his open contact lens case, one contact still floating around in the clear solution. It is brown. Why in the world is the contact brown?

"Why are you wearing colored contacts?" I ask, glancing toward my husband, who is still fiddling with the first lens he placed into his right eye.

"What are you talking about?" He sounds annoyed as he places his finger into his eye, ever so lightly.

"When did you start wearing colored contacts?"

"I have worn contacts all my life."

"*I know that*, but not colored."

"I have always worn colored contacts, Katherine."

He glances toward me as he spits out the words, seemingly offended at my lack of contact lens knowledge. The stark contrast of his one brown contact lens and one blue eye take me by surprise.

"You don't have blue eyes." I state stubbornly.

"Yes, clearly, I do. I have always worn colored contacts."

"I don't understand. I have never seen you with blue eyes, and I have definitely seen you without contacts in."

"Obviously not."

"Why would you cover blue eyes?"

"I prefer the way I look with darker eyes."

I stand there, staring at my husband's reflection in the mirror as he places the second contact lens into his apparently blue eye. I think back to the last twelve years of our relationship. I know Billy does *not* have blue eyes. Surely, I would have noticed that at some point in *twelve years* prior to now. The man has *always* slept in his contact lenses, but I must have seen him without them in before…right?

Billy goes about his business, as if that was a completely normal conversation. He gets into the running water of the shower and I stand in front of my sink, staring into the reflection of my own amber brown eyes. I think back to a conversation many years earlier, when our marriage was still very young, when the topic of future children stayed on our tongues.

"I hope they look like you." I said, staring lovingly at the boy Billy had once been.

"Well, we know they will have dark eyes, like us both…but I hope they get your red hair." Billy replied.

If Billy has the dark eyes I remember, then who is the blue-eyed man currently naked in my shower?

Chapter Four

The day passes quickly as I clean and prepare food for dinner tonight with the Millers. While I enjoy spending time with Lucy and her husband, I find myself wishing I could postpone. I need to figure out what is going on with Billy, but I can't exactly tell anyone my concerns. What would I even say? I'm pretty sure I killed my husband, but then I woke up to him lying next to me in bed? Now I think it's not even Billy…it's some imposter whose taken his place?

I sound crazy just thinking any of this.

I knead the dough for the dinner rolls I will serve tonight and stare at the cross hanging above our mantel. I should feel shame for what I did. What I dreamt I did?

Whether it was real or a dream murder, I feel no shame at all. I did the right thing for us both.

Divorce would be a black stain on our lives, a burden on our loved ones. Friends and neighbors would be expected to choose sides, to suddenly shun the other party. Our friends have intertwined, been involved since we met in high school. How could we expect them to cut those ties?

A woman being abandoned by her husband, never to hear from him again. A husband going missing, never to be found. A woman in her early thirties becoming a widow…those things are tragic. Those are the kinds of things that bring a community together.

Divorce would tear it apart.

No, I did the right thing for everyone. I rub my flour covered hands on my apron and cover the dough to rest. Well, at least I thought I did the right thing for everyone.

The soreness and aches my overworked body felt, the leftover lasagna, the suddenly blue eyes. These things can't be coincidence.

As I wash my hands, I glance out the bay window overlooking the backyard. The shed door sits slightly ajar, the lock hanging loosely from the metal clasp. I grasp a kitchen towel in my hands and find myself remembering the night of my husband's murder. The hours spent dragging the sled which carried his lifeless body, digging a pit that felt endless. I was exhausted. Exhausted like I had never known the word before.

As I dragged the empty sled out of the woods, I felt delusional with exhaustion and sleeplessness. I brought the sled to the shed, telling myself I would carry it to the loft, where all our rarely used gear and decorations reside, the next morning. I was so tired, I forgot to lock the shed. It must have been me. I rub my hands dry on the kitchen towel and exit the mudroom door, heading toward the shed.

I swing the door open, cringing at the loud creak of the rusty hinges. I step inside and pull the string hanging from the center of the room, the lightbulb flickering a few times before solidly lighting the dank space. The large, black, plastic sled lay at the foot of the ladder leading up to the loft. I run my fingers along the edge, hoping to trigger some undeniable moment in my memory that could explain how the dead man in my house could be so alive.

Nothing comes to mind.

I heave the sled above my head and push it up the ladder, following behind it until it is securely in the loft once again. As I lay it to rest in its usual spot, I notice the dirt smears and leaf pieces clinging to the underside track.

I climb down the ladder slowly, my high heels making the endeavor more frightening than it should be, and leave the shed, locking the door securely behind me. Instead of returning to my baking, I walk to the edge of the woods, my eyes tracing the barely recognizable drag marks the sled tracks left in the soft dirt.

The soreness and aches my overworked body felt, the leftover lasagna, the suddenly blue eyes and the clearly used sled.

Everything is pointing to me killing my husband.

Everything except the fact that my husband is very much alive.

Chapter Five

Billy and I sit beside each other, staring at Lucy and Stevie Miller, seated across from us, a perfectly laid dinner table between the pairs.

"This roast is delicious." Lucy chirps happily, a forkful of pot roast entering her mouth shortly after.

"Thanks Luce, it's an old recipe. How are the kids? Is Cassie doing girl scouts this year?" I ask, doing my best to seem interested.

"They are both wonderful. Yes, she will be shaking you two down for cookie orders soon enough." She shakes her fork toward us, a small sliver of beef swinging wildly from one of the prongs.

"I look forward to it." Billy said, chuckling. "I love thin mints."

I glance at my husband, unable to hide the puzzled expression on my face.

"What?" He asks.

"I thought you hated mint." I bluntly state.

"No, not at all." He chuckles again, quickly starting conversation with Stevie.

His casual dismissal gets under my skin. I'm starting to feel like I don't know my own husband. I guess that's what happens when he is replaced by an imposter. This is crazy. Billy doesn't have a clone. My husband is sitting beside me, not buried in the woods. I don't know why my memory is messing with me, but I clearly did *not* kill my husband. It must have been a dream. Or maybe I really am losing it.

"Kiki, are you okay?" The sound of Lucy's voice reminds me that I am not alone.

"Yes, yes, of course." I say quickly, grabbing the basket of rolls and silently offering more bread to our guests.

It is obvious that Lucy knows something is off. Something is wrong. More than likely, she is questioning if there are problems in my marriage. The marriage that looks perfect from the outside. Any married person knows that is never the case. A marriage is never perfect. I'm okay with whatever ideas about my marriage are currently swirling around my neighbor's brain. I would rather that than the truth. I can't exactly tell her the man beside us *isn't* my husband. If I did, I would have to admit to murdering the real Billy.

New Billy's laugh brings me back to reality and I wince at the cutting sound. That is not the sound I have heard since high school. Anyone would remember a cackle like that.

I force myself to focus and ensure the perfect façade I have become the master of wearing is intact. I can't let on to anything being too wrong. Minor marriage troubles are normal. A wife losing it will be the talk of the town…and the last thing I need right now is more eyes on me.

Chapter Six

After the neighbors leave, I stand at the kitchen sink washing this evening's pile of dishes. I take advantage of the alone time and get lost inside my own brain.

At first, I thought the murder of my husband must have been nothing more than a very detailed dream. I know better than that. I know the things I have done in preparation of this. This was no crime of passion. This was a tiny seed planted in my mind, watered daily and tended lovingly until it sprouted into murderous action.

Six months ago, I began my serious planning. The seed had sprouted and started to take over every sliver of space inside my head. I couldn't avoid it anymore. I knew that the only way I could be free of these thoughts, would be to act.

Initially, I found joy in the quiet planning. Entertaining the idea of taking charge of my life for the very first time. Billy's death never felt like the end goal, it was simply a necessary milestone along the way. The true goal has always been freedom. I have never actually known freedom in the way that allows you to find yourself.

Billy and I started dating in high school, at the encouragement of my parents and our pastor. Our families were both very active in the church, of equal social status, and hopeful for many, many grandchildren. My life had been planned out before I even began to dream about my own future. I followed what those around me wanted, assuming they knew what was best for me. It was the way I had been trained; I see that now. My parents had trained me to be in the back seat of my own life, never the driver. I don't even think it was malicious. Simply, what they believed was best for me, or maybe all they really knew.

While I gave in to the encouragement about dating, and later marrying, Billy…I silently protested the idea of children. It isn't that I never want to be a mother, but the idea of pumping out a baby every year like I am some kind of procreation factory simply disgusted me. Shortly after marrying, I did the first thing for myself that I had ever done. Birth control. I am still thankful for that decision every day. For a long time, that small daily protest was enough to make me feel like I had some form of control.

Then something inside me broke. Some dam that had been holding back millions of liters of water, the small cracks that had formed over many years suddenly giving way. The silent protest wasn't enough anymore. I needed freedom, not in the sense of being imprisoned or captive, but in the sense of choice without restraint. Over the years, I had begun to associate my lack of freedom with the decisions that had been made for me, the life that had been created around me, placing me inside like a tiny doll inside the perfect little dollhouse. Billy was the biggest of those decisions.

He had to go.

Divorce has never been an option.

But if Billy suddenly disappeared, I would be free to have my own life.

I would still be the perfect doll in everyone's eyes, just another choice made for me while I sat idly by.

Chapter Seven

A perfectly clean house and well-fed husband. That is what has always been expected of me. A good little housewife's duties. *It's your job to make him think the sun comes up just to hear him crow, Katherine.* It has been a long twelve years of marriage.

I stare at a sleeping Billy while I lie awake wondering where I went wrong. Not so much of the how did I get here line of questioning…no, I now see what being a marionette has done to my life. There's no getting back that time. More along the lines of why am I still living the exact same life I planned to destroy? How did my plan end up so badly?

It is clear that I have committed murder. There are far too many signs, shining so brightly it is nearly blinding in the darkness of my life. Yet, here is the man who I have murdered. He is lying next to me, breathing in the air that should belong to me. I should end him right now and let this all be over with. But, would it be over? Would he actually die? Clearly, I have reason to question it.

It's not like the man is a zombie. I shiver at the thought. That would be terrifying actually. Suddenly wanting to be further away from the man sleeping too peacefully for my comfort, I rise from our bed and pad down the stairs toward the kitchen. I fill the kettle and wait for the water to boil. Mindlessly reaching into the cabinet above the stove, I select my favorite tea without even comprehending what I am doing. Some things become so routine.

Once the water has boiled, and the tea has seeped its requested three minutes, I stand at the sliding glass door staring into the backyard. My fingers wrap around the hot mug and my toes wiggle against the chilled floor. The shed now closed securely, the lock perfectly in place. My eyes wander to the wood line, the trees swaying slightly in the light breeze. The leaves dance so subtly, it almost looks like the trees are breathing. I stare into the woods as deep as my eyes will allow, hoping to trigger some new memory.

The swirling thoughts all come to the same conclusion I have tried to avoid these last few days. I have to go back into those woods.

I have to dig up my husband's body.

Chapter Eight

The tie on my robe knotted as tightly as I can pull it, I slide on a pair of flats and tip toe as quietly as I can out the mudroom door. The last thing I need right now is zombie Billy waking up. I don't know that I will be able to explain anything about what I am on my way to do. To anyone.

The grass is slightly damp and rubs against the exposed tops of my feet, leaving a slight film in its place. I feel immediately dirty being out here in my pajamas.

As I approach the shed, I pull the key from my robe pocket and work the lock silently. I pull the door open only large enough to squeeze inside, hoping to avoid the squealing sound of its creaky hinges.

Navigating this mess of a shed in the dark is frustrating, but it is not the first time I have done it. I just hope that it is the last.

After feeling around the dark workbench drawer for a minute, I locate the sharp edge of a hand shovel. I remove it, running my fingers along the tool for confirmation of my findings. I pocket it, the wooden handle sticking out against my hip bone, knocking against me as I navigate my way back outside.

A deep inhale later and I step into the woods. The memory of my recent trip in this exact spot fills my mind as I walk, my own promise already broken. *I will never set foot in these woods again.* I had practically chanted it silently as I dragged the empty sled back to the shed. An immediate sickness, guilt and shame, had swirled in my stomach. Fear had made plenty of appearances too. Maybe this is my second chance? Maybe I am not the killer I thought I was during that walk back to the shed. Maybe it is all some sickness inside my own head and I never did any of these unthinkable acts at all. All of it nothing more than wild hallucinations, alerting me to my own need for help.

The walk feels endless, miles seemingly passing beneath my feet. I hadn't picked out a specific spot in my planning; I just stopped where it felt right. It has to be getting close. I slowly scan the ground as I walk, looking for the tell-tale sign of recently upturned dirt. The consistent thud of the wooden shovel handle against my hip bone has started to irk. I grab the handle to still it, stop it from its constant reminder of what I am about to do.

A large area of dirt, slightly darker than the dirt surrounding it comes into view and I stare suspiciously, almost waiting for some form of movement. Deep in my gut, I know this is the spot.

Suddenly, I am on my hands and knees, stabbing the shovel into the dirt and throwing it from the fresh mound. I become as animalistic as the act feels, practically growling as I uncover my kill. Desperate for answers and praying for none at all. Speckles of dirt fly around my head, covering my robe and finding its way into my hair. In this moment, I don't remember that ladies aren't supposed to get dirty. I don't remember to be careful with my fresh manicure, or that the caked dirt and mud will clog up the washing machine.

I don't remember that proper ladies don't kill their husbands.

I simply remember exactly how my husband looks dead.

The blank stare of his brown eyes, completely unbothered by the dirt now sprinkled across his pupils. His full lips slightly parted, as if he may speak again at any moment. The deep baritone voice filling the forest and relieving the tightness in my stomach. The sickening pale, gray tone of his skin, a new addition since I had last seen him.

As his face comes fully into view, lying in the hole, right where I left him…he is very much, dead.

Chapter Nine

The defeated walk back to the house felt much quicker, and more terrifying, than the walk in. I left my husband lying dead in a hole in the woods behind my house. It is not some dream, or wild hallucination. It is my reality.

I am a killer, and there is an imposter in my bed.

The realization is more terrifying than the fact that I am a murderer. There is a man pretending to be my husband. *Who would even want to be Billy?* He looks just like him, except for his blue eyes. He speaks like him, the deep voice that warms your ear canals and makes you believe he is the leader in every group. He even has the same mannerisms and talks about the same interests. How could this man be a stranger and yet so familiar?

As I glance at the stove clock, registering that it is nearly time for fake Billy's alarm to wake him, I move stealthily upstairs and click the bathroom door closed behind me. I quickly ball up my dirt caked clothes and shove them into the bottom of the hamper. I run the shower as hot as it will go and stand under the water, hoping to burn off so much more than just skin. A few minutes pass and I hear a soft knock on the door before it begins to open.

"You're up early." Imposter Billy says.

"Yes, I figured I should get a jump start on my baking for the church bake sale on Thursday." I reply from behind the shower curtain. I can't look at this man right now. I don't know if I am more scared of the Imposter, or the confirmation that everything in my life will now change. *This is what I wanted. This is what I needed.*

"Sounds like a good idea." He answers curtly.

Did he know that I was gone? Had he heard me come into the bathroom? Did he lie awake wondering where his fake wife had gone? Or had he seen me appear from the woods that now houses my husband's corpse?

The sink water begins to run and I hear his shaving brush clinking against the glass bowl holding the shaving soap.

I scrub my skin in the scalding water, listening to the scrape of the razor against the Imposter's face. Who is this man and what exactly does he want from me?

Chapter Ten

After dressing for the day and serving a breakfast of scrambled eggs and waffles, I watch Billy's car reversing down our driveway as the Imposter leaves for work. Once the car is out of view, I race up the stairs into the bedroom I now share with this stranger. I start with his nightstand, ripping open the drawers and rifling through the various junk inside. There must be something here to give me some sort of lead about who this is.

I open the ring box that typically housed Billy's wedding ring, the ring he stopped wearing years ago, claiming he just wasn't a jewelry type of guy. I roll my eyes at the memory. I wonder if that was the moment he knew this marriage was nothing more than a legal transaction we found ourselves trapped in. The two of us had never spoken of divorce, the mere utterance of the word would have been a sin in this household. I often wondered if it was as prevalent in Billy's mind as it was in mine.

I lift the box, running my finger along the edges, feeling suddenly nostalgic. I lift the lid and am met with the empty black velvet lining. Where is Billy's ring? He had begun wearing his ring again?

I close my eyes and try to picture his hands. The image of my own fingers wrapping around his limp, slightly hairy hands, pulling with all my power, slowly sliding his large frame onto the waiting sled. The sled that would bring him to his unmarked grave. I would have noticed his ring on his finger…wouldn't I? I place the ring box back into the drawer. Somehow, the idea of Billy deciding to wear his ring again makes the guilt of my crime boil hot in my stomach.

Finding nothing else of interest in the nightstand drawer, I swing the closet door open and glance around, finding nothing obviously out of place. I begin to squeeze the pants and jackets hanging in front of me, suddenly hearing the soft crunch of paper. I unzip the pocket of the worn black leather jacket and reach my hand inside, pulling receipt paper from the pocket.

Unfolding the paper, I find an expensive meal at a swanky local restaurant that I have certainly never stepped foot in.

The Tortoiseshell Table opened last fall, a high scale, trendy restaurant with overpriced dishes and unbelievably beautiful staff. I begged Billy to go, hoping for a romantic date in a world that I have never felt a part of, and he laughed. He laughed then ranted for ten minutes about how gullible I must be to fall for the hype of some restaurant with mediocre food at astronomical prices. He always found a way to make me feel even smaller than I already did.

Yet, here it is. A receipt in his jacket pocket, dated nearly two months ago, for a bill that could not have been for just one person. I sit on the edge of the bed, feeling suddenly defeated. Clearly, Billy must have been right. I was quite gullible. Not for wanting to have a unique experience at an overpriced restaurant with the man I made vows to, but because I believed those vows meant as much to him, as they did to me. I didn't even like Billy as a human being, but those vows are a promise. A promise only one of us kept, apparently.

Was Billy cheating on me all this time? His sudden refusal to wear his ring years ago should have alerted me to something being off. Have I spent my life so absorbed in the illusion of a perfect marriage, that I never actually took part in this marriage at all?

I crumple the receipt in my fist and stuff it back into the jacket pocket. I hate to admit that the idea of an affair still hurts. I literally murdered this man and I'm pissed at him. I almost laugh at the absurdity of it all.

I continue my search and find nothing to give me any details about the identity of fake Billy. I leave the bedroom feeling more confused than when I entered, and resign myself to beginning my baking.

Chapter Eleven

On the morning of the church bake sale, I set the table and carry the tray of pancakes into the dining room. Billy is seated in his usual chair, the same chair he took his last breath in. *Maybe it's a sign, maybe this Billy should take his last breath there too.* I place the dish in the center of the table, directly next to the plate of sausages.

"Would you like orange juice, or just a refill on your coffee?" I ask. Meals with Billy had become so routine, I don't even think before the words leave my lips.

"Sit down and eat. I can get my own coffee." Imposter Billy says, standing from his seat and pulling out my chair in one swift motion.

I stare into those brown contacts, feeling incredibly suspicious. I almost ask what the hell he is doing. There must be some ulterior motive to this.

I was not abused in the way that people condemn. Billy never hurt me physically, he never called me names or put me down. But I don't think he ever actually showed me love. I don't think he ever actually felt that. It was always a show, a façade carefully orchestrated for everyone around us.

The real Billy…dead Billy…would never serve himself. He would never concern himself with my need to eat.

"Okay…" I whisper, sitting in the offered chair, but never taking my eyes off of the man calling himself my husband.

I watch as he walks into the kitchen, pouring himself a refill of coffee, then returning to the seat beside me.

"No need to wait for me, go ahead and eat." He says, sipping his coffee and leaning back in his chair.

It suddenly hits me that this isn't niceties. This is suspicion. New Billy must know that I murdered the real Billy…does he know how? He must. He must want to make sure I am not poisoning him too.

I silently place a pancake on my plate, buttering it slowly and pouring a thin line of syrup in a circular motion. The perfect target of syrup now sits atop my pancake. I take my time, making a show of it for the Imposter's watching eyes. *I know that you know,* I silently convey. As I take my first bite, I chew slowly, swallowing and allowing my lips to curl into a smile that doesn't meet my eyes.

"Delicious."

Fake Billy emits a small sigh, as if he truly expected me to drop dead from a pancake. I nearly roll my eyes.

We eat silently, watching each other suspiciously.

I stand from the table, piling the dirty dishes together and carry them to the kitchen sink. I begin the familiar mundane task of washing the breakfast dishes and feel a presence behind me. I turn quickly, seeing Billy looking alarmed.

"I'm leaving for work. Thank you for breakfast." He says, leaning forward and kissing my cheek tenderly. "I will see you at the bake sale."

"You're coming to the bake sale?" I ask, forgetting my surprise at the kiss.

"Of course. I want to support my wife. The world-renowned snickerdoodles are just another benefit." He smiles warmly, and I am taken back by how genuine he seems. Is this how a normal husband would treat his wife?

I guess I wouldn't know.

"Okay. I guess I'll see you there." I say, unsure how I am supposed to respond in this moment.

Clearly, this man may look exactly like my husband, but he certainly didn't know the inner workings of my marriage to Billy.

I stand in front of the sink, listening to the mudroom door close. I rub my cheek absentmindedly, waiting for the sound of his car engine to cease.

Chapter Twelve

"Kiki, over here!"

The sound of Lucy's voice rings through the local high school's gymnasium. I glance toward the sound, finding my petite neighbor waving her arm excitedly, her overly white smile acting as a spotlight to guide me to the table.

"Hey Luce!" I try my best to match her energy, hoping to avoid the 'are you okay' question tonight.

I set down the large box nearly covering my view, then set down the tote bags full of Tupperware containers swinging from my already full arms. I smile at Lucy and exhale deeply, feigning exhaustion from carrying in a truckload full of baked goods, when the fatigue I am feeling has nothing to do with endless snickerdoodles.

"Perfect timing! I just finished getting my stuff all setup. This is your half of the table; I'll help you lay everything out." Lucy says, gesturing to the bare side of a long dingy plastic table.

As we uncover plates of snickerdoodles and gingerbread cakes, we make small talk about our church and lightly gossip about its members. As much as I like Lucy, our relationship is quite surface level. She is great to giggle and gossip with, great to sit next to in church and share a bake sale table with, great to invite over for dinner or drinks…but have I ever actually confided in her about anything meaningful in my life?

Have I really confided in anyone?

Maybe if I had, I wouldn't have gotten to this point. I would certainly never trust her with a secret as big as murder. In some ways, it is nice to feel an escape when I am with her. In Lucy's eyes…I *am* the façade I have been perfecting all these years.

"Has everything been okay lately? You seemed off at dinner." Lucy asks quietly, glancing around to ensure none of these nosey church women can hear us. Everyone is busy setting up their own tables.

"Yes, of course. Everything is great!" My voice squeaks slightly on the lie, making it sound so forced. I clear my throat, gently touching it as if to indicate the problem is physical, not emotional. I reach for the bottle of water I brought in one of the tote bags and take a long sip, watching Lucy eye me suspiciously.

"Okay…well, you can always talk to me whenever you need a friend."

"I appreciate that, Lucy. I will absolutely take you up on that whenever it is needed." I smile again, smoothing down the skirt of my dress. "Would you like a snickerdoodle? Free of charge for a wonderful friend."

Lucy smiles briefly, grabbing a cookie and pretending to focus on the other tables in the room. Maybe it is my fault that our relationship has never deepened further. It's easier to maintain a lie from a distance. I guess my marriage taught me that.

I glance out a nearby window, watching strangers park their cars, crossing the parking lot, walking toward the building in search of delicious sugar filled treats. A familiar stranger comes into view, the man pretending to be my husband walks across the parking lot.

Instead of heading toward the building in search of snacks, he is walking toward the football field, a single vehicle parked near the grass. His footsteps quicken as he approaches the vehicle, a beat-up white truck, and yanks on the passenger door, climbing inside. *What is he doing?*

Minutes pass as I stare at the white truck, burning its details into my memory…the tinted windows, the lone stick figure sticker on the driver's side of the long back window, each of the dents and scratches covering the body. The real Billy had very few friends, if any. I think he expected me to handle the social aspect of his life, as well as pretty much everything outside of his career. Apparently, this Billy likes to support his 'wife' *and* has friends.

"What are you staring at?" Lucy's voice breaks my attention.

"I think I forgot something in my car." The lie comes out quickly, my legs jumpstarting into action before she can reply.

The click clack of my high heels echoes off the lockers lining the empty hallways as I rush toward the parking lot. I don't know what I am planning on doing exactly, but I need to at least get a look at the driver of the white truck. Maybe this is the puzzle piece I need for the enigma that has become my life.

I crack the heavy door open slowly and peek outside, scanning the parking lot and finding the white truck still sitting in the left corner. The window tint prevents me from judging who, if anyone, is inside. The truck is at least close enough to my own car that I can use that to my advantage. Hopefully that dang tint won't make this whole thing pointless.

I inhale and exhale deeply a few times, prepping myself to act natural, then walk outside into the darkening parking lot. Willing myself to walk at a natural pace, I focus on the sound of my heels and find it soothing to my pounding heart. The truck is in my eye line, but I do my best to pretend I don't even notice its presence.

I approach my own car, opening the back driver's side door and stealing glances toward the truck in between pretending to look for some lost item in my back seat. My knees pressed into the fabric, I run my hand around the underside of the seats, staring at the truck now a mere seventy-five feet away from me. If I didn't see a light smoke emitting from the muffler, I wouldn't even know the car was occupied.

How long can I pretend to look for something that doesn't even exist? I'm sure they have seen me…maybe fake Billy is now waiting until I go back inside before he leaves the truck. I mean, that's what I would do.

I scoot myself backwards slowly, my leg searching for the ground behind me. I might as well go back inside; I'm convinced we are just waiting each other out at this point.

My feet find the ground and I lower my head, trying to avoid my hair getting ruffled. I may be a mess inside, but that's no reason to look a mess on the outside… that's how I get the town talking. The last thing I need right now is more eyes on me.

"What are you looking for?"

The sudden baritone voice behind me causes me to jump, bashing my head on the car door frame. I step backwards, rubbing my scalp gently and trying to stop the sudden stars in my vision.

"Sorry, I didn't mean to startle you." Imposter Billy says.

Where did he come from? I have been watching the truck and never even saw the car door open. He is sneakier than I realized.

"Well, maybe don't sneak up on me then." I hiss, still touching the top of my head tenderly.

"Sorry. I wasn't thinking." He says, reaching out to touch my arm. "Are you okay?"

"I'm fine." I lie. "Let's just go inside, I need to get back to my table."

We begin walking, me smoothing out my hair and skirt, feeling suddenly self-conscious.

"What were you looking for?" He asks again.

Who cares what I was looking for? He knows that I came out here to watch him. Unfortunately, I guess I am just not as sneaky as this man is.

"I can't find my favorite lipstick. I thought maybe it fell out of my purse in the car."

"Oh. What color is it?"

What am I, in a police interrogation? This man is irking my nerves, and I already feel a headache coming on. He thinks he can get the better of me. I have been lying about my entire life for as long as I can remember. I may be terrible at surveillance, but lying is my specialty.

"It's Revlon. Called Toast of New York. It's a red with some minor brown undertones."

I know my lipsticks. The lie comes so naturally. This man really thinks I can't name sixty lipsticks in under a minute flat? Please. I *know* lipsticks.

"Oh."

We walk in silence the rest of the way to my bake sale table. Once there, I plaster a smile on my face and address Lucy.

"Look who I found in the parking lot."

"Hey Billy!" Lucy's electric white smile brightens the whole room, and I see the mild surprise on her face. I guess she knows Billy well enough to know he would typically skip something like this.

"Hey Lucy, what sugar are you pushing tonight?"

Lucy starts talking about the treats piled in front of her, obviously excited to have interest in her hard work. I can't help but stare at this man in front of us. He may look exactly like my husband, but his personality will be his downfall. Billy would never even feign interest in something he considered women's work. I'm realizing he was kind of a pig.

The Imposter points at Lucy's banana walnut muffins, asking some question that I can't seem to focus on. The white gold band around his ring finger catches my eye and I realize that he is wearing the ring I bought for Billy nearly thirteen years ago. I feel a warmth spreading in my chest and find myself happy to see it.

I should have known Billy didn't suddenly start wearing it after leaving it in his nightstand drawer for years. It somehow suits this stranger's hand better anyway. Billy's fingers had become fat, squeezing the metal from both sides and looking like his finger was being strangled. This man seems made for it. At least someone is enjoying it, I guess.

Chapter Thirteen

A night of fitful sleep, and dreams filled with that beat up white truck, left me feeling exhausted as soon as my eyes peeled open this morning.

I smeared extra concealer under my eyes and chose a deep red lipstick, meant to draw the eye away from my tired under eyes. After I unrolled my hair curlers, I pinned one side back and let the auburn curls flow freely down my back. I feel like hell, but that's no excuse to look like it. My mama was the same way. It has been ingrained in me for so long, I can't remember a time I didn't wear a dress, high heels and lipstick. It is all part of being a good wife, according to my mama. *The moment you stop dressing up for your husband, that's the moment his eyes will wander, and who could blame him? No one wants to marry a hog, Katherine.* It is so ingrained in me; I guess I actually believed it. At least until my late-twenties, when I realized wandering eyes have everything to do with the man you married, and nothing to do with the woman wearing the ring. By the time that realization was made, I was already set in my ways as far as my dress code went. Besides, it's all part of the masquerade that is my life.

Fridays are the day I go to the market. As much as I want to follow fake Billy and see if he is actually going to work, I know it is important to keep up with my normal routine. In a small town, you'd be surprised just how many people know your routine.

The employees at the grocery store will notice if I am not there today. Who will ask Taylor in the bakery how her infant son, Elliot, is doing? Who will stop by the meat counter and talk to Mitchell about his dream of opening his own butcher shop? And during checkout, Jackie is expecting me to giggle at her latest date night stories. I am as much a part of the weekly happenings at the market as the weekly shipments of fresh produce from our local farmer, Glen.

Fake Billy will have to wait. I will do my usual weekly shop, attend to each of my market regulars, then

I will check on what the stranger wearing my husband's wedding ring is doing.

I leave the market feeling incredibly drained.

The simple act of forcing a smile is difficult when you feel like both an offender and a victim. It is all a complicated dance along a very fine line. I am a murderer, and the Imposter must know that. He has something on me that forces me into silence. On the other hand, he too, has a dirty secret, likely more than just one.

What would drive someone to take over a dead man's life? Is he on the run from the law? Did he know Billy? Maybe he is out for vengeance, carefully plotting my demise, planning to bury me deep in the woods, an unmarked hole next to my rotting husband.

I unclench my bloodless knuckles from the steering wheel and lock my seatbelt across my waist with a click. I shake my head lightly, hoping to bring myself back to reality, and reverse out of the parking spot slowly.

The drive through this tiny town is so familiar to me, the same roads I learned to drive on are now the roads that take me to Billy's workplace. I was never meant to live such a small life. Die in the same place I was born, spend my entire life following everyone else's plan. I *know* I am meant for more.

Six months ago, my little Lexus sedan drove this same road, heading out of town for a very different reason. I like to drive this road, pretending my commonplace sedan is actually a 1955 Dodge La Femme, a beautiful cream and pink symbol of housewives demanding a presence beyond the term homemaker. It feels like such a fitting car for me.

As I had done each time I ventured out of the town where everyone knows me, I stopped at a run-down gas station in the middle of nowhere. A place that only truckers go for a bathroom break and to stretch their legs. A place that has more dead roaches than patrons. A place that wouldn't dare have cameras.

There were times that I met some very seedy individuals in this parking lot. The type of people willing to assist in getting rid of a woman's husband, for the right price. I considered passing off the job to someone else entirely, but let's face it. I don't have money. The money I have resides in a joint account, easily noticed by the person now lying under a few feet of dirt.

I considered slowly saving, taking small bits of extra money that wouldn't be noticed. The change from groceries, the tithe money meant for the church. Somehow, that thought made me feel worse than the idea of killing my husband.

A man I met in this very parking lot was the one who gave me the idea I was looking for. The perfect solution to my problem. My idea of a payment plan laughed off by him, he instead gave me an option I had never considered.

Hemlock.

A poisonous plant, easily added into someone's food, known to cause respiratory failure relatively quickly. This, he was willing to provide me for nothing more than a favor. No money involved.

I should have known better than to owe a man like that a favor.

Chapter Fourteen

I pull into the parking lot of Billy's office building and glance around the front, making sure that the Imposter is not standing outside. I slowly drive up and down the rows of cars, looking for the familiar SUV. The black Tahoe comes into my view as I approach the fourth row of cars, and I continue driving by as if looking for a parking spot.

So, he is here.

Fake Billy has somehow stepped into the real Billy's career as effortlessly as he sleeps in my bed. I don't even understand what a Data Analyst does, so more power to him.

I park my car in the adjoining row and wait a few minutes, ensuring no one is around. I drove all this way; I might as well get a look inside the car.

I turn my key ring to the spare Tahoe key and walk nonchalantly toward the driver's door. I shove the key into the door lock and turn it quickly, glancing over my shoulder again. I really don't want to be snuck up on again by the familiar stranger. I don't think he will believe I drove all this way to check his car for a lost lipstick.

I slide into the car, closing the door quietly. I am immediately hit by the smell of old food and sweaty socks. I cover my nose with one hand and search the center console with the other. What is this man doing in here? He's had this car for a week and it already smells like a frat house.

I sift through the stuffed cup holders, finding gas station receipts and fast-food wrappers. I crawl onto the seat, my knees facing the rear of the vehicle, and thrust myself over the center console, straight into the back seat. I'm thankful no one was around to see the clumsiness of it, my skirt surely showing more than I ever intended. I smooth back my hair, using the rearview mirror to ensure nothing is out of place.

A lone duffle bag sits on the floorboard of the back seat, and I quickly unzip it and begin to sift through a pile of dirty clothes. Clothes I have never seen. At first, I assumed it was a gym bag, but I am realizing the outfits stuffed into this oversized duffle are anything but gym clothes. I pull out a pair of jeans and reach my hand into the pocket, feeling my palm wrap around something hard and something paper.

Suddenly, a deep voice booms from a distance, and I realize it is new Billy laughing. Daring to lift my head slightly, I peer through the windshield, seeing the Imposter talking to another man as he is getting into his vehicle. They are a mere two rows away from me.

My heart pounds hard in my chest as I quickly rezip the duffle bag, again glancing out the window. The man is in his car now and Billy is walking this way. I open the back passenger door slightly, praying that fake Billy's attention is on anything else right now. I slide out the door, my heels making way too much noise as they hit the pavement. I duck and close the door very gently.

I don't dare move. I can't see where the Imposter is, and I get the sinking feeling that I may be getting snuck up on again.

"Billy!" An unfamiliar voice. "Why don't you just come to lunch with me? We'll go up to that restaurant at Route 60 and Cookie Road. I hear the waitresses are hot, man."

A forced laugh that is entirely too close to me. He is standing at the driver's door. "Maybe another time, man. I should call my wife."

"Aw, come on, man. You can text her on the ride there. I'll drive."

Silence.

"I'll pay, man! Come on! I've never had to convince you to look at hot waitresses before."

"Alright, man, alright. You're right."

I remain completely still, listening to the sound of footsteps waning. A car door slams and an engine revving. I exhale deeply, the adrenaline catching up to me. As soon as the sound of the engine proves the car is out of the parking lot, I stand, smoothing the skirt of my dress.

I want to run to my car, locking myself inside the safety of its interior. Instead, I casually walk toward the sedan, unlocking it slowly, checking over my shoulder before I sit inside. It is only then that I remember my hand is still wrapped around the contents of Billy's pocket.

I open my fingers to reveal an orange lighter and a small scrap of paper. I set the lighter into the center console and return my attention to the paper. It is crumpled tightly. I carefully unwrap it from itself, smoothing it with my thumbs. An address appears.

"1983 Bearpoint Drive"

Why does that address sound so familiar?

The buzz of my phone nestled in the cup holder causes me to jump, and I angrily grab it. A text message from Billy's phone.

"Hey honey, thinking about you."

Is this really how fake Billy thinks the real Billy was? It's almost like he is trying to get me to ask who he really is, or maybe he knows exactly what he is doing. Maybe he wants to remind me exactly where the real Billy is.

"Thinking of you too, my love!"

I smirk as I hit send. I can play this game too, Imposter.

You think you need to remind me where my husband is.

Maybe I need to remind you who put him there.

Chapter Fifteen

The Imposter has presumably gone to lunch with his pig of a coworker, and now I have this familiar address courtesy of his dirty jeans. Where do I know this address from? I open my phone and plug it into the GPS, it never coming up in my history. Only a sixteen-minute drive from my current location, I decide I might as well make the trip now.

As the voice of a British woman navigates my directions, I get a tiny feeling that I have been to this location before. Why else would it feel so familiar? I head further away from town, through vast expanses of unused land that looks like nothing more than big piles of dirt and sand.

As I begin to see signs of civilization again, my GPS alerts me to an upcoming right turn. The neighborhood sign looks worn, various weeds and overgrown plants slowly creeping their way toward the words 'Pallo Coppers'.

That nagging feeling of familiarity is taking over again and I almost feel myself guiding the car to my destination without the aid of GPS.

The neighborhood itself seems as worn as the sign that welcomed me in. The homes I pass don knee length grass and broken shutters. Nothing to say that it is abandoned, more just a lack of the love these homes deserve. Cars fill the driveways, and in some cases the overgrown yards. The GPS continues to navigate, sending me deeper into the neighborhood that feels familiar, but distant.

Finally, an end to the street I am navigating is in sight. It isn't a cul-de-sac, but simply an end to the street, as if the pavers just ran out of asphalt and decided it was good enough.

The navigation continues to guide me straight and I slow the car to a crawl until I realize the dirt and overgrowth in front of me is actually a very worn, nearly impossible to notice, driveway. This place doesn't even have a mailbox so I have no idea if this is the correct address, and I feel incredibly awkward as I meander toward what I hope is a home, and not some terrifying trap.

The overgrowth seems to consume my car whole within a minute and I realize that not even the neighbors would see that I am here. What if Fake Billy knows that I have been snooping? What if he put this scrap of paper in his pocket on purpose, thinking I would eventually find it and be unable to keep myself from coming here? I wonder if this is his real home, and I am about to be the next girl he chains up in his basement…basically hand delivering myself to this monster.

I am removed from my troubling thoughts at the sight of the home before me. Unlike most of the homes I passed through the neighborhood, this one seems to be in near perfect condition.

A single-story rancher made of red brick with black shutters that are definitely not broken. Even the white paint used for the trim seems to be fresh and dirt free. If you disregard the yard from hell, this home could be in any middle America neighborhood. I wonder if all the homes in this neighborhood once looked like this, before everyone collectively decided to stop caring.

It does seem odd though, that someone put so much love and care into this home, but allows the yard and driveway to become a jungle.

There are no cars in the driveway as I park and decide to look around. I have to figure out why I have this nagging feeling that I have been here before. Instead of getting snuck up on, I decide to knock on the front door first, at least make sure no one is home. If they are, I'll just pretend I'm doing door to door petitioning, or selling internet services or something. Do people still sell makeup like that? I could definitely fake being an Avon lady.

I walk the red brick pathway up to the front door and get a sense of déjà vu. Why do I know this place? I allow the buried memory to form in my mind and I see Billy standing next to me on this porch, ringing the doorbell. The house looked different back then.

It was some holiday, wasn't it? I glance down at my memory induced self and remember the ugly Christmas sweater Billy insisted that I wear. It was a Christmas party, and we were still dating. I must have been barely out of high school. In my memory, the front door swings open and I see a burly, bearded man in a comically feminine red Christmas sweater, sparkles glittering in the light and green bow strings dangling around him.

Uncle Ted.

This is Billy's Uncle Ted's house. Of course. I had only been here once before, and it was over a decade ago, but I am certain of it now. Nearly seven years ago, Uncle Ted passed away suddenly, leaving Billy to take care of his estate. Ted had no children, no spouse and really only one asset, this house. Billy took care of the whole thing, telling me he was just going to put it on the market as is and take the first offer with no pushback. The house sold quickly and I hadn't thought about any of it since.

Realizing I am still standing on Uncle Ted's porch, and that the house is owned by someone else now, I snap back to reality and ring the doorbell. I still need to figure out why Fake Billy would have this address, and honestly, I've been standing on this porch too long to just turn around and walk back to my car like some weirdo. I have to pretend to sell something, at least be a weirdo with a purpose.

I tap my foot, listening to the muffled echo of the doorbell chime. I glance around, feeling incredibly awkward and somehow not alone. The stillness of nature will do that to you. I ring the doorbell again, knocking loudly as well. I have to be sure no one is home.

After another few minutes of silence, I peer into the small windows by the front door. The interior hallway looks exactly as I remember it, apparently the new homeowner likes the musty yellow color Uncle Ted had chosen.

I walk the exterior of the house, careful to choose a path not consumed by tall grass. I stop at each window, peering inside, though the blinds prevent me from actually seeing anything.

As I near the driveway, I stand on my tiptoes to peer into the last window. Instead of being met with the obstruction of blinds, I find myself staring into the master bedroom. The layout of furniture hasn't changed, though the comforter looks much newer than the dated pattern Uncle Ted had.

I remember staring at the thick fabric, the muted green background and delicate florals and bold geometric patterns of Ted's bedspread, it all clashed and worked so well together somehow. I remember thinking maybe that is the perfect metaphor for Billy and I. If the bedspread could work, so would we.

I remember being unable to look away, my eyes tracing the strange patterns as Billy's voice hissed angrily.

"You've had two drinks; you are done for the night. I don't need some drunk girl to babysit, or my family to think I would bring *that* type of girl home. You need to dial it back too, and quit encouraging my uncle with his insane conspiracy theories. Honestly, I could hear you laugh across the room. What are you, a hyena? Act like a lady, for God's sake. I don't know why I have to teach you how to be a lady. Ridiculous."

We weren't even married yet and I was already broken. No wonder he wanted me as a wife. I was nothing more than a meek lump of clay in his hands. *How could that be what my parents wanted for me*?

The new bedspread, a lovely sage green quilted pattern seems to soothe the eyes, so unlike the wild calamity in my memory. I admire the cleanliness of the room, and realize the new owners seem to be minimalists with classic tastes. It doesn't seem that they have put any money into upgrades, no replacing aged carpet or even a coat of fresh paint, but it seems clean and loved.

As I brace myself to step back from the window, I glance at the bedroom door, my eye catching on a large framed photo next to it. An aged photograph and frame, many smiling faces filling the large picture and my guts suddenly twist.

It is the same photo that hung beside the bedroom door the night Billy privately scolded me. The night that should have set off a million red flags, but instead made me feel like I needed to do better. The night that I first learned I would have to put on a façade to please Billy.

The young toddler Billy smiles up at the photographer, surrounded by his extended family and a wave of nausea hits me.

I don't know if it is from staring into the eyes of the child that grew into the man I murdered, or if it is the realization that Billy couldn't have sold this house, but I turn and vomit into the overgrown bushes scratching angrily at my tights.

Chapter Sixteen

A desperate urge to get away from the house has me nearly squealing my tires as I leave the driveway, a cloud of red dust in my wake. A thousand questions swirl around my head and I can't shake the feeling that I may throw up again.

Uncle Ted died nearly seven years ago. Billy said he would handle everything, and just two months later, the house had sold. At the time, it was in need of updates and some repairs, so we never expected much money from the sale. I never even asked how much it sold for; it didn't really seem like my business and the last thing I wanted was to give Billy a reason to get annoyed. Clearly, he couldn't have sold it. What kind of person would have a family photo of the previous homeowner hanging on their wall? No one. Literally no one would do that.

Okay, so Billy didn't sell the house. For seven years he had been hiding that fact. While the yard seems to be in complete shambles, the house looks like it is well loved. He has clearly done repairs and some upgrades to the outside, at least. Why would he be putting money into this house? Maybe he planned on slowly repairing and upgrading, hoping to get the most out of the eventual sale? But why the new bedding in the master bedroom? It was as if he was living here.

Regardless of whatever Billy was planning for this house, the more pressing question on my mind is why Fake Billy had this address scribbled on a piece of paper in his pocket? Did Real Billy and Fake Billy know each other? I feel sick. I press the gas pedal harder, wanting to be out of this neighborhood as quickly as possible.

As I turn onto the main road that will lead me back to the safety of my tiny little bubble, I start to think about what kind of life Billy lived. I did everything that was expected of me. I was obedient and meek. I let the script of my life be written by those around me. I was powerless because I gave them that power.

Billy, on the other hand, was the sole author of his script. He never had to change or better himself; he never had to do a single thing for the benefit of anyone else. I find myself daydreaming about what that must feel like before I realize that *I* am now my own author.

That is the gift I gave myself when I murdered my husband.

Chapter Seventeen

The drive home emboldened my newfound rebellion and I embrace the reality of no longer being Billy's wife. I run the bath water as hot as our water tank allows and squeeze half a bottle of bubbles into the running water. It is there that the Imposter finds me an hour later, still soaking and skin pruned.

"Oh hey, I didn't hear you get home." I say lazily, feeling entirely too relaxed for someone who just murdered her husband and is now living with a man pretending to be him.

"There you are. I was surprised to not find you in the kitchen."

"I'm not making dinner. I don't feel like it." Words I never thought I would utter. Words my new found murderous freedom have created.

"Okay, want me to make you a sandwich?"

I sit up in surprise. No harsh words. No push back. No judging that the lack of a hot meal makes me less of a wife. If I had any doubt about the body in the makeshift hole in the woods being a figment of my imagination, this conversation would put an end to that. This man is *not* Billy. And I'm realizing how much I like that fact.

"Yeah. Extra mayo."

"You got it."

The better Billy leaves the bathroom. I hear him whistling as he descends the stairs. I resign myself to finally ending this bath and watch the water swirling down the drain for a few minutes before I dry off.

If I could convince myself to play pretend the rest of my life, I may just stop my questioning all together right now and settle in to a possibly better marriage with Billy 2.0.

Unfortunately, I have played pretend for long enough.

I don't want to keep living my life wearing a mask. But I am no fool. This isn't as simple as just asking who he is. We both know I'm a killer. We both know he's an imposter. There must be a reason he is doing this.

As I dress, I try to come up with a clever way of asking about Uncle Ted's house. I decide against it, since I am still unsure of too much. I need to play my cards close to my chest.

"One ham sandwich, extra mayo and pickles." The Imposter slides the plate toward me, now seated at the kitchen island.

"How did you know I love pickles?" I ask.

"We've been married long enough for me to uncover your secret pickle addiction." He winks, a devilish grin on his lips. The words escape so naturally, I almost let myself believe them, for just a moment.

I giggle. Okay, so maybe it's not some big secret, but honestly, this man has known me all of a week and a half. How could he know how I like my sandwiches?

The thought strikes me so suddenly I nearly choke on my mouthful of deli meat…maybe he hasn't only known me less than two weeks. Maybe our introduction was not him sliding into bed beside me, post homicidal rage.

I mean, he had to have seen the murder, right? Or possibly just Billy's body being dragged through the woods? Either way, he knows Billy is dead. Which means he was watching. Had he been watching our house? Had he been waiting in the woods, watching my deepest secret unfold as the mound of dirt my shovel created became higher and higher?

"Are you okay? Are you choking?" The sound of his voice brings me back to the present.

"Yes, yes, I'm fine. Thanks."

We eye each other suspiciously for a moment, him surely wondering if I am capable of eating food without supervision. Me, wondering if this man had been stalking Billy long before I brought about his death.

Chapter Eighteen

The following morning, I accept my now routine kiss on the cheek before the man, now known as Billy, leaves the house.

It is Saturday, which means that Billy goes to the hunting lodge for a few hours after breakfast. I know the Imposter is keeping up with Billy's schedule, but it suddenly dawns on me that it's possible Billy never went to the hunting lodge at all. Maybe it was just another excuse to live the life he preferred, away from me.

I scrub the breakfast dishes more viciously than intended and decide that the first chance I get, I need to get my hands on Billy's key ring. There must be a key to

Uncle Ted's house, and I have searched our room as thoroughly as if I had a warrant. It must be on that key ring, since it is never alone with me. I need to get inside that house. If Billy was keeping it, and ensuring I had no idea, there must be a reason.

After pining back my curls, I reapply my lipstick and decide that I can't wait around at home for fake Billy to come back. Normally, I basked in this extra time to be alone. Today, I feel too anxious to enjoy anything. I need answers.

Fifteen minutes later I am in my car, driving that same road leading out of town toward the Binmay Hunting Lodge. I have never visited Billy here, which may turn out to be a good thing, considering the parking lot is tiny and I am likely to be seen by someone. I don't know what I'm planning on doing once I get there, but I can't just sit at home hoping the answers fall into my lap.

A quick loop around the compact parking lot tells me that Billy's car is not here. I sigh heavily, realizing I am probably right that he never even came to this lodge. I decide it can't hurt to ask around, at least I can have one answer for my troubles.

As I walk into the small log building, an overwhelming smell of damp wood hits my nostrils. I wasn't expecting much from the size of the building's exterior, but I am still shocked by the grimy interior I am now standing inside of. An elderly man at the counter gapes at me, eyes wide and judging. I get the feeling I am the first woman to ever grace this building with her presence.

"Can I help you, Miss?" His voice sounding sturdier than his fragile frame had led me to expect.

"Hey there!" I pause to smile sweetly before continuing. "I'm lookin' for my husband, Billy. Is he here?"

The old man's gaze seems to soak me in, lingering just a moment too long in all the wrong places.

"You just missed him. Said he had to leave early for a lunch with his brother."

Brother? The real Billy was an only child. The only child for an entire generation of that family, actually. His aunts and uncles never reproduced and his mother had a very difficult pregnancy with him. She decided she was blessed enough to have one, and to not push her luck. I guess this stalker didn't do as much research as I thought.

"Oh shoot. I thought we were going to ride together. Do you know where they went?"

"He didn't say. We were all just so happy to have him back, it slipped my mind to even ask."

"Of course. It's been so long, I mean, what has it been now? It feels like forever."

The man chuckles and nods his head in confirmation. "Yes, yes, it does. Must have been a few years now, at least. He kept paying his dues, though."

I bet he did. The perfect alibi for Saturday mornings away from your wife.

"Yes, he didn't want his membership to lapse. This place just means so much to him."

If he can hear the sarcasm in my voice, he doesn't let on. My statement seems to invoke a bit of pride in the man and I decide to get out of here before I have trouble biting my tongue.

"Well, thank you so much, sir. I should really give him a call before I'm late for lunch. I hope you have a blessed day."

"You too, ma'am."

I leave the parking lot quickly, scanning the nearby lots for the Tahoe. If he is actually having lunch with someone, he must be nearby. It's not like there are many choices of restaurants in a town of a few hundred people.

It only takes ten minutes before I spot Billy's vehicle. I enter the parking lot to the only Thai restaurant in our town and park at the far end, away from the view of the restaurant windows. The Tahoe is parked near the front of the lot, a white pickup truck just one row behind it. A white pickup truck with a lone stick figure sticker on the driver's side of the very tinted back window. It is the same truck that met Billy at the church bake sale. I can't believe my luck.

I try waiting patiently for about ten minutes before I realize that surveillance is absolutely terrible. How do police officers do this? The minute you are still with nothing to do, you have to pee desperately and are simultaneously absolutely starving. The Thai food smells delicious. I glance at the clock and realize it is almost lunchtime.

I try to let my phone distract me for a bit, but I can't take my eyes off the restaurant's front door for too long, or I might miss them leaving. I check in the rearview mirror that my hair and lipstick are intact, then pull out my compact and lightly powder my face. Just because I am stalking two strangers doesn't mean I shouldn't look my best.

I suddenly hear my mother's voice echo inside my head, her southern accent slightly stronger than mine is now, *A woman only needs to worry about a few things in life, Katherine. One of them being your looks. If you don't care about lookin' ugly, then why should your husband care about his eyes wandering?*

She did that a lot…tied my worth to my looks. *But where did that get us, Mama*? I wake up every day, do my hair and makeup, put on a beautiful dress and only take off my heels for bed, and my husband was probably still cheating. *What do you blame for that, Mama*? I'm sure it would be something else I am doing wrong. Everything always comes back to the woman.

I click my compact case closed and slide it back into my purse just as my target is opening the building's front door. Fake Billy and the man in the white truck appear to be deep in conversation, but it looks anything but pleasant. Billy looks worried, the man in the truck just looks angry. I find myself sliding down in my seat, even though neither man has so much as glanced in my direction.

They walk toward the cars, arms flailing animatedly and lips moving full speed. Imposter Billy approaches his car door first, turning to say a goodbye to the angry truck driver. I am caught off guard as they hug goodbye, nothing to sentimental, more the type of hug that men do to other men they are very close with.

Maybe this is the Imposter's brother? At the very least, a close friend. Does this man know that the Imposter has taken Billy's place? I wonder if he is in on whatever scheme the Imposter is trying to pull here.

A few more minutes of waiting and both the men are in their vehicles and pulling out of the parking lot. In a spilt second, I make my decision. I have to follow the white truck. I have to know who the Imposter's brother really is.

Chapter Nineteen

The man in the white truck is not a good driver. I guess I shouldn't be surprised considering the number of dents and scratches all over his car. Luckily, the streets are never full of traffic in Starfire, Texas, so I can keep a good distance while still having a perfect view.

I follow behind for what feels like an hour. Where are we going? I had assumed the white truck would lead me to his house, or at least somewhere that would prove useful, but I am starting to wonder if he knows I am following him. What if he is purposefully getting me far away from home to do something terrible to me?

Sure, I am a killer, but I just poisoned the man I pretended to love. I'm not sure if I could actually use physical violence against someone else. If I could, it wouldn't be this guy. He would easily overpower me.

The truck finally begins to deviate from our seemingly endless journey, about two miles after passing a sign indicating we are now in Bearios, Texas, turning right onto a dirt road. The sign at the front of the road indicates it is a neighborhood, Fox Greens.

I continue driving straight, looking for the next opportunity to turn around. I want to give white truck enough time to park and go inside whatever house he is going to. I have to make sure he doesn't see me snooping around. For all I know, white truck knows exactly what the Imposter is doing, and knows exactly who I am.

The area has become quite rural, so I drive for another ten minutes before I finally come upon an area that is safe to turn around. At least I feel confident that I have given enough time to not be seen inside of Fox Greens.

As I approach the neighborhood, I sigh deeply, feeling suddenly nauseous with worry. *Please don't let this be a trap.* As my tires enter the dirt road, the cabin begins to shake with the rough terrain. Tall trees line the road, hiding what is in store for me ahead. It all feels so ominous, but I force myself to stay focused. If anything goes wrong, I will just drive full speed out of here.

The thicket of trees begins to thin and a line of trailer homes come into view. I glance to each side of the road as I drive, looking for the familiar white truck. The neighborhood is larger than I expected, and I spend some time going up and down each street, each of them branching off the main road and ending in a cul-de-sac.

As I drive down a street named *Westport Way*, I suddenly see the familiar dents and scratches covering the body of a white truck. It is the sole vehicle parked in the front yard of a run-down, aggressively blue trailer. The yard is littered with tires and various trash, making the trailer look much worse than it actually is. It may be unloved, but it doesn't look abandoned.

I drive the street normally, turning around in the cul-de-sac, and deciding that I have to take this opportunity. I know now where the white truck man likely lives…but what does that actually mean? I don't know who he is, I don't know why he is meeting with the Imposter. I really don't have any answers. I can't go home with nothing.

I drive past the home, stopping my car far enough that it would be unseen through the windows of the blue trailer. He may know my vehicle already, but if he doesn't, there's no need to give him any information. I walk down the unpaved street, my legs wobbling slightly with nerves. I wipe the sweat blooming on my palms onto the skirt of my dress.

As I cross into the yard, mere feet from the white truck, I feel suddenly struck with the realization that I have nothing to say to this man. Why am I doing this? What am I going to say? *Hey, I killed my husband then woke up to your friend in my bed…who is he?*

Before I can even create a plausible lie, the front door swings open hard, the bang against the wall making me jump. The man who met the Imposter for lunch stands on the little front porch, a brown beer bottle dangling from one hand.

"Who the hell are you?" His gruff voice is anything but welcoming. He is larger than I realized, his tangly mess of a beard hiding the entire lower half of his face.

"Hey there!" I smile nervously, trying to buy time while I figure out anything to say.

"What the hell you want? Why're you on my property?" He grips the neck of the beer bottle tightly, reminding me that it could easily become a weapon, not that he would need it against me.

"I just wanted to talk to you, if I could." I say meekly, hoping to portray that I am no threat to him.

"You some reporter?" He says harshly, eyes narrowing accusingly.

"What? No, no. I am not a reporter."

"A cop, then?" This time his voice sounds threatening.

"No, I'm not a cop."

"You have to tell me if you're a cop."

"I'm not a cop." I repeat.

"Didn't fink so. You don't look like no cop. You look like a reporter, though." He chugs his beer, never taking his eyes off of me as I watch the bottle drain.

"Why would a reporter come talk to you?" I ask.

At this, his body stiffens, the grip on the surely empty beer bottle growing tighter.

"You tryin' to trick me? You think you're so smart, huh? I knew it, a fuckin' reporter. Didn't I tell y'all to stay the fuck off my property? Get! Get outta here!" As he speaks, the anger in his voice deepens with every word.

Before I can react, he swings his arm wildly, throwing the beer bottle. As the bottle smashes against the truck, pieces of glass graze my bare arm. I grab my arm instinctively, and turn quickly, wanting to be out of here before he gets even more upset.

It isn't until my heels hit the dirt street that I turn around, seeing the man's arm raised toward me, his middle finger saluting proudly. He smiles devilishly and goes back inside his home, slamming the front door so hard I'm shocked the hinges are still intact.

What is his problem?

I rub my arm and start walking down the street, toward my car. The feeling of defeat washes over me and I realize I now have even more questions and even less answers. I stop, turning again toward the offensively blue trailer and see no sign of the man. The door is still closed, and the blinds are closed tightly on the front windows.

I can't leave like this. I can't go home with no answers. I can't keep playing pretend with an imposter.

I scurry back toward the house, my eyes never leaving the windows. As I approach the yard, without even realizing what I am planning, I creak open the plastic mailbox and grab the envelope sitting on top of a rather large pile of mail.

I turn quickly, my heart pounding against my ribcage so aggressively, I think I may be having a minor heart attack. I grip the letter tightly and try my best not to break into a full speed run back to the car. I don't want to draw any extra attention, but my heart is pounding so loudly, I am not even sure I would hear that crazy man running up behind me.

Relief washes over me as I sit in my driver's seat and hit the lock button. *I am safe.* I glance down at the envelope now wrinkled from my grip.

Nikolas Palmer.

I have a name…and names bring answers.

Chapter Twenty

Once I am out of the neighborhood, I drive faster than I normally would toward Starfire. I have never missed my little hometown so much. I glance at the stolen envelope now laying on my passenger seat. Isn't stealing mail a crime? A federal crime, I think. I swallow hard, trying not to imagine myself sitting in a prison cell.

Maniacal laughter escapes from my lips and I find myself unable to stop. Tears stream down my cheeks and my jaw muscles become tender before I can pull myself together. I am more worried about stealing mail than I am about murdering my husband. The smile remains on my face and a feeling of relief washes over me. I didn't realize how much I needed that laugh.

The relief is short lived as my phone pings, alerting me to a new text message. The number is not saved in my phone, but it is familiar. My stomach lurches and I quickly open the message.

Meet me.

Short. Simple. No details.

Yet, terrifying.

I hold the message with my finger, selecting the like option to acknowledge the request. Not request, really…more like demand.

I knew I would have to pay up eventually. *A favor.* It's all he wanted in exchange for the hemlock. Nothing to tie me to any poison, nothing illegal done. Just two people exchanging a completely legal, completely poisonous plant. Sure, I could have just grown it myself. I just didn't want any tie to me. I didn't want it growing anywhere that could be easily accessible to me. Nothing to even suggest that I could have had anything to do with it.

The placement of his body is not ideal. Of course, it is much too close to home. I had no way around that for the moment; he is much too heavy for me to move elsewhere.

Originally, I had planned to let him decompose enough to be easier to dispose of. Or at least, enough to attract animals. The man who now texts me for a favor offered to dispose of the body in a way that no one would ever find him. I have no idea what that means, and I prefer to keep it that way.

I declined. Not because it wasn't a tempting, and much needed, offer. Simply because I did not want anyone else involved. I don't want anyone to be able to testify against me with real evidence, should it come to a court case in the future. No, I will handle this.

Besides, the man wanted a favor for simply providing me a legal plant. What would he want to dispose of a body? I shudder at the thought.

I desperately want to go home, but I know that I have to do this. I just don't know exactly what *this* is.

I pull into the run-down gas station parking lot, parking in my usual spot in the very back, hidden from both the roadway and the shed sized convenience store.

The tall, lanky man in the oversized black hoodie steps out from the hedges, as he always does. I have no idea what he drives, or where he comes from, but it is unnerving every time. He walks toward my car and I step out slowly, dreading that my time for payment has finally come.

Chapter Twenty-One

"Hey." I say to this man who knows my darkest secret, yet doesn't even know my name.

"Everything go okay?" He asks, and I know what he means. *How did the murder go? Is your husband six feet under?*

"Something like that." I mutter, not wanting to tell this stranger the impossible to believe situation I am currently in.

He grunts, seeming to accept my response without any further questions. I guess when your business involves shady answers, you learn not to question things any more than necessary.

"You needed a favor?" I ask, hoping to get this interaction over with quickly.

While I found it so easy to confide in this stranger during my most desperate and lonely times, I am finding it hard just to be in his presence right now. This man, who undoubtedly has killed an unknown amount of people, is making my guilt burn red hot. The Imposter has allowed me to pretend my darkest sin never happened. This stranger reminds me that I will never be free of my own actions.

"Yeah. No questions, though. Just do it."

I gulp. Something about that statement, coming from this man, makes me instantly terrified. What exactly is he going to ask me to do? Does he want me to *kill* someone for him? He could do that himself, couldn't he? Why would he ask a housewife to handle such serious business? Maybe he wants me to be his drug mule. I am *not* putting drugs up *there*, if you know what I mean.

I turn to see him watching me, his eyes such a dark brown that it is impossible to distinguish the iris from the pupil. Pock mark scars cover his cheeks, and a small linear scar runs through his left eyebrow, reminding me of that trend where people shaved a notch in their eyebrow. People did that to look tough, I assume. I wonder how this guy got the actual scar.

"I need four dozen cupcakes. Different flavors. Whatever is good."

I burst out laughing. I can't help it. His face pinkens and I only lose myself deeper in the laughing fit.

"I'm sorry." I finally manage to say. "It was just unexpected. And I have so many questions, but I won't ask them. Of course, I will do it. When do you need them by?"

"I need 'em on Tuesday morning. Real good too, not the store-bought crap."

"Understood. I can definitely do that."

He nods solemnly and heads back toward the hedges, disappearing to some unknown hideout.

I rush toward my car and breathe a sigh of relief as I leave the parking lot. I have no idea what this guy is playing at, but this is a favor I can actually do.

Chapter Twenty-Two

I arrive home to find that Billy's car is still not here. Strange. Maybe I should have followed the Imposter. I grab the envelope off the passenger seat and shove it deep into the inner pocket of my purse. At least I have a name to look into, today was definitely not a waste.

Once inside the house, I begin preparing dinner. With the cottage pie in the oven and wannabe Billy still not home, I start googling the name Nikolas Palmer. Luckily, his first name has a less common spelling but it is apparently still a pretty common name. Pages and pages of results load, the first page completely taken up with news articles. I glance at the headlines and my eyesight seems to blur as I try to make sense of the words.

I click on the first article titled *Brother of Missing Woman Named Person of Interest.* The article's main picture shows a tall, curvy woman, her skin dewy and glittering, her smile so warm and inviting. She is absolutely beautiful. I skim through the article, seeing a man named Nikolas Palmer had been named as a suspect in the disappearance of his sister. I continue scrolling until a small photo comes into view in the middle of the article. A heavier set man, broad shouldered and muscular, his dark beard covering the bottom half of his face in an unkempt pile of wiry hair. A smile that is unknown to me, a face that is burned in my memory.

Nikolas Palmer.

The man in the white truck.

Chapter Twenty-Three

After the realization that the man in the white truck is the same Nikolas Palmer in this news article, I read the entire piece in full. No wonder he accused me of being a reporter, or a police officer. He is likely harassed by them both since becoming a person of interest.

Nikolas' sister, Marnie Palmer, went missing just a few weeks ago. She was last seen by her brother the morning of the day she vanished, which makes him a person of interest. Apparently, she stopped by the ugly blue trailer to bring her brother freezer meals she made him for the week. According to Nikolas, she then left for work. Her boss stated that she never arrived.

What in the world is fake Billy doing hanging out with someone who is probably a suspect in a murder? I mean, he sleeps beside one every night now, so I guess he has a type. What if he is trying to hire this guy to take me out? Get revenge for the real Billy. I giggle at the ridiculousness of it all. I complained I was bored, that I never truly got to live my life. Maybe I was better off being bored.

I close out the browser and pull the cottage pie out of the oven just as the Imposter walks in the mudroom door.

"That smells delicious." He says as he kisses my cheek. It has become our routine form of affection, and I admit that I am starting to find it sweet.

"Thank you. How was your day?" I ask as I begin pulling out plates and silverware to set the dining room table.

"Good, good." He remarks. He sounds distracted as he stares out the kitchen window, toward the woods. I wonder if he knows he is staring at the place where the real Billy's body lies decaying.

He snaps out of his fog and grabs the pile of dishes from my arms. "Here, let me do that."

He then strides toward the dining room, leaving me in the kitchen feeling stunned. In the near thirteen years of living in this house, I don't think anyone else has ever set the table. I stand in the middle of the kitchen, unsure what to do with this newfound free minute.

I move to the sink and stare toward the woods, Billy now fresh on my mind. I never considered that Billy was not a good husband. I blamed so much of this result on being bored in my marriage, on my whole life being planned and never making any choices for myself. I see now that every reason, every excuse I gave myself, put all of the blame on me. I put on this façade of a perfect marriage, a perfect life, and I think the only person that ever fell for the lies…was me.

The Imposter has done nothing but treat me with the most basic respect and kindness. How is it that a stranger has shown me more of those things than Billy ever did? My marriage to Billy mirrored my parents' marriage in so many ways, that I never even considered that it may not have been normal. It may not have been healthy. Is it possible I am better off with an imposter?

If only it were that simple. I dispose of one husband and a new and improved one appears by the next morning.

No, this man is here for his own reasons. He is not some knight in shining armor here to show me how a woman should be treated. I can't lose sight of that. He is not my husband.

The clank and clatter of dishes as the table is being set brings me back to the present. I pull out my phone from my apron pocket and search the name *Marnie Palmer*. The missing woman's lovely face fills the search results and I can't help but feel connected to her. She exudes warmth through a photograph, and I find myself wondering if we would have been friends. What kind of life did she live? She probably didn't feel trapped in a life created by everyone around her. She probably stood up for herself more than I ever could. An irrational sense of jealousy floods me momentarily.

I scroll down the results, passing the first page filled with articles talking about her brother Nikolas. Earlier articles appear, calling her husband a person of interest as well. So, she was married. She must have kept her own last name. That alone tells me she was so much freer than I could ever imagine. Billy probably would have refused to marry me, had I even suggested keeping my maiden name.

I select one of the articles randomly, hoping to learn more about the woman who feels like someone I want to know. I skim the page, a typical story of a husband under suspicion when his wife mysteriously disappears. *It's always the husband*, they say. In my case, it was the wife. I can't help but smile.

As I approach the middle of the article, a new, smaller picture comes into view. It is the husband of this lovely woman. I stop scrolling, my finger paused midair, eyes burning a hole in the screen. The olive skin and straight light brown hair are familiar without being exact. The blue eyes strikingly distracting. The nose is so obviously different, throwing off my brain's ability of recognition. Despite my momentary confusion, I know this face.

"What are you reading?" Fake Billy's voice surprises me, making me jump and nearly drop the phone in my hand.

His eyes bore into me and the silence between us seems to swirl around me, wrapping itself snuggly around my neck, my chest tightening and breathing becoming rapid.

The lighter straight hair now dark and wavy, always slightly messy, the way Billy's hair had been. The blue eyes, now darkened by brown contact lenses. The once large, crooked nose, now straightened and carved into a manageable size, mirroring the nose Billy had been born with. The familiar face designed to mirror the man that now lies in a makeshift grave in the woods beyond my house.

The Imposter is Marnie Palmer's husband.

So, what exactly does he want from me?

Chapter Twenty-Four

The following morning, I sit in the fourth row of pews from the front, listening to the pastor's sermon halfheartedly. It has been a week now since Billy has begun rotting. The Imposter sits beside me, as Billy had always done, seeming to listen intently. Max Jameson, formerly known as The Imposter, remains a person of interest in the disappearance of his wife, Marnie Palmer.

After an awkward dinner last night, I managed to lock myself in the bathroom long enough to google the hell out of Max Jameson. Everything I found involved Marnie's disappearance, and it all made me more suspicious of his presence in my life. Is he running from police by taking the place of my dead husband? I considered immediately going to police, but what exactly would I say? *I know that man isn't my husband because I killed him and buried his body in the woods behind my house. If you need proof, just go dig up his worm-infested corpse.* There's no option here that would allow me to maintain any innocence. This is the perfect cover for Max, a man running from the law.

So instead, I sit beside Max Jameson in the same pew I have spent every Sunday service in since I was a baby. The hardest part of it all, is pretending that nothing is wrong. Pretending that I know nothing at all, and that I actually believe this is my husband. We both know partial truths. I just have to keep playing this game long enough to figure out Max's end goal.

This has all been quite the distraction from Billy's death, and I feel a bit annoyed that my freedom has again been postponed. As the reality of being free from Billy begins to set in, I am realizing what kind of man he actually was. I glance toward Max, the side of his cheek rough with stubble, his attention still unbroken. Why would this man *want* to be Billy? I wonder if Billy even wanted to be Billy.

I glance down at my hands, interlaced tightly in my lap. Guilt creeps up my throat. I should be listening to this sermon. I should be begging for forgiveness and mercy. An entire lifetime of my beliefs lay before me and I just can't muster enough energy to pretend that I feel the need for forgiveness. I am not sorry for what I have done. I feel more guilt for being lost inside my head instead of showing this sermon the attention it deserves, than for murdering the son of a bitch that called himself my husband.

Does that make me a terrible person?

I may be struck down right here in this pew and I would stand before Him admitting these exact words I only whisper inside my head. Billy was a horrible husband and I was a shell of a wife, giving in to the routine and choices laid before me, never questioning, never feeling.

I have woken from the coma of my life.

And I am glad the corpse named Billy has no one left but the worms wiggling through his gore.

Chapter Twenty-Five

After returning home from church, we fall into the typical routine of dishes and football. Once I am finished, and begin tidying the rest of the house, Max finds me aggressively scrubbing his bathroom sink filled with yesterday's beard hairs.

"I need to run over to the Hunt Club; I think I left my sunglasses there yesterday."

I have never seen the real or fake Billy wear sunglasses, but this is clearly an excuse to get out of the house for some secret reason. Sounds like the perfect time to follow him.

"Ok darling, drive safe."

"Thanks, I will." He leans down and kisses my cheek lightly.

As he leaves the bathroom, I decide to lay it on nice and thick. "I hope you find your sunglasses! I know how much you love them!"

He stops momentarily and mutters a quick "thank you" before continuing his mission.

I throw the scrub brush into the sink and quickly wash my hands. After hearing the mudroom door close, I rush down the stairs, grab my purse from the counter and crack the blinds in the dining room. I watch Billy's car back out of the driveway, Max at the wheel looking determined.

When I am sure he cannot see the mudroom door from his rearview mirror, I dash to my car and reverse out of the driveway a bit too quickly. I nearly hit the mailbox in my haste, and softly swear, then whisper my thanks that I don't have to make up some story about a wild gang of teenagers out for mailbox vengeance.

I drive entirely too fast for the neighborhood, and hope I don't hear complaints from the neighbors later, but knowing them, it will likely just be whispers behind my back. That will have to be fine, whispers are the least of my worries right now. As long as they don't contain the words, *she killed her husband*, then I really can't waste any worry on them at the moment.

As I approach the traffic light to exit the neighborhood, I see Billy's SUV completing the left turn, and the light in front of me switching to red. I cut off another car to get in the right lane, wait until I am clear and make a right turn. I get into the left lane and U-turn at the next neighborhood opening.

I see Max ahead of me and keep enough distance to avoid being spotted. If I had any tiny hope that he was actually going to the hunting lodge to look for lost sunglasses, that hope is quickly dashed. He navigates his vehicle in the opposite direction of the lodge, instead pulling into a shopping plaza.

I purposely slow as I approach the traffic light, forcing myself to be stuck at a red as Max enters the plaza. I watch his vehicle like a hawk while I wait for my turn to enter. He parks near the hardware store and quickly exits the SUV. The flash of green in front of me alerts me to my turn, and I enter the parking lot carefully, never allowing Max out of my view. He crosses the road toward the hardware store front door as I find a parking spot near the little market next door.

I quickly follow the path he has laid out for me, and pray that he is not looking at something near the front door when I enter. Luck is on my side as the little bell dings, alerting the shop keeper to my entry. I smile and wave in greeting, making sure not to say a word in case the Imposter is already familiar with my voice. I glance around to find two shoppers walking the nearby area, neither of them Max.

The click clack of my high heels against the tile floor seems to echo off the walls, alerting the entire store to my existence. I feel like I'm walking around with a spotlight beaming down on me, a ringmaster with a megaphone announcing my arrival. *Presenting the woman who killed her husband! Behold as she stalks the imposter who has taken his place!* I know my life has become a circus act, but I'd really prefer to avoid an audience right now.

I round the corner of an end cap carefully, peering into the upcoming aisle, and quickly pull back. I press my body against the end cap and breathe deeply, willing my heart to slow down. I peer slowly again, Max's back coming into view as he pushes a cart down the aisle, away from my newfound hiding spot. He halts, staring up toward a shelf, seeming to consider something about the product in his eyeline. His muscular arm reaches onto the shelf, pulling a flat blue package toward himself, then throwing it carelessly into the cart. *A tarp.*

Once Max has left my sight, I rush down the aisle, praying he doesn't suddenly realize he forgot something and turn around. As I reach the end, I again peer slowly around the end cap and see that he is now continuing his shopping in the next aisle over. The previous end cap faced the back of the store, and I quickly become aware that I do not have the luxury of cover from this spot.

In a dress, heels, and enough makeup for a photoshoot, I stick out like a sore thumb in these aisles littered with men in their paint covered overalls. Couple that with the behavior of an inexperienced stalker, and I have drawn more than a few unabashed stares.

Another glance around the end cap and I see that Max is no longer in view. I again walk swiftly down the aisle, slowing toward the end to glance around the end cap. A gasp escapes me as Max's back comes into view mere feet from where I stand. I squish myself against the merchandise, feeling a burst of adrenaline like a child about to be punished for disobeying her Mama. Why am I so jumpy? *He* is the one who lied to me. I can easily pretend I needed more batteries or super glue. *He* is the one who will have to explain why he isn't at the hunting lodge.

Feeling emboldened, I steal another glance, just in time to see Max abandoning his cart and entering the bathroom in the back of the store. I watch as the door closes, a loud click emitting as the lock turns. I scurry toward the cart, desperate to see the contents before he returns.

A blue tarp.

A crowbar.

A rope.

A roll of duct tape.

A gas can.

A pack of zip ties.

This cart is a murder kit. This man literally watched any murder documentary in existence and used it to write out his shopping list.

The sound of the water running snaps me back to reality and I rush back to the aisles he has already visited. He isn't a murderer, right? Murderers don't wash their hands after they pee, surely? I feel like the kind of person who is willing to kill someone probably doesn't worry about hand washing.

Then I remember I am a murderer. I probably look like the furthest thing from a murderer…yet, my hands are permanently stained with sin.

Is the Imposter planning on killing me? I am the only one who knows he isn't the real Billy. It would make sense that he would want to take me out…tie up the only loose end in his little plan. But what exactly *is* his little plan?

Chapter Twenty-Six

I leave the hardware store before Max has finished his shopping, having decided that I have seen enough. That is the most suspicious shopping cart I have ever seen in my life. It is clearly being pushed by someone who has or will commit murder.

Panic begins to overtake me at the realization that I am not safe. Of course, he has been nothing but kind to me…he wants me to put my guard down. What was I thinking? This man is an imposter! A stranger who has forced his way into my life in the most unbelievable way. I have always been suspicious of him of course, but I need to be ready to protect myself. This man is dangerous.

I rush home before Max can return, and begin prepping for dinner to keep my shaking hands busy. As Max enters the mudroom, I am rolling out the dough for a pie crust. His empty hands mean the murder kit must have been left in the car.

"Are you making a pie?" He says after gently kissing my cheek. Everything in me begs to pull away and I nearly shudder as I suppress my instincts.

"Yes, apple." I respond curtly.

"Wow, that's amazing." He sounds genuinely impressed.

I bite back a sarcastic remark, reminding myself that I have to play the game. He can't be alerted to anything different.

I smile sweetly, trying my best to look flattered by his comment. "Oh, it's nothing." I say, waving my flour covered hand.

"Don't brush it off. It really is impressive; you are amazing in a lot of ways."

I stop rolling the dough and lock eyes with the Imposter. Why is he suddenly buttering me up? No one has ever spoken to me in this way and I am frozen with the surprise of it. I feel embarrassed by his words, but much more concerned about the motives behind them.

"Okay." My voice comes out meek and I feel my skin burn red with shame. The last thing I want is to come off as weak to this man. *I killed a man, damn it.* I shouldn't be scared of anyone. *He* should be scared of *me.* I could kill the Imposter, too. There's plenty of woods behind the house. I could dig a second hole.

I clear my throat. "Thank you." I say, my voice exuding much more confidence this time.

The rest of the day follows the same boring routine that has filled the last twelve years of my life. The only difference is the large hunting knife I found in Billy's closet and slid under my side of the mattress. I keep reminding myself not to be scared of this man…that *I* am the killer. It doesn't hurt to be prepared though. In a fight, strength will not be on my side…but this knife will be.

Chapter Twenty-Seven

The intrusive beep of Billy's alarm clock grates at my brain for a full three minutes before Max finally shuts it off and gets out of bed. He seemed to sleep peacefully beside me all night, while I stared at the ceiling long enough to count higher than the world's population of sheep.

No matter how exhausted I felt, my eyes refused to remain shut longer than a blink. The knife underneath the mattress seemed to burn red hot against my back, reminding me of the reason that it lay waiting.

I release a sigh from deep in my belly and force myself to begin my day. I will need a little extra time for my makeup after a complete lack of sleep. Some affirmations are probably most needed today, but I skip that wishful thinking and head straight for a hot shower. Lucy's squeaky voice fills my brain, *the worst days are the best days for affirmations…it really works, if you do the work, Kiki!* I grunt, a scowl on my face at the Lucy inside my head. Do boundlessly positive people ever annoy themselves? Or just the rest of us?

The heat from the shower swirls around me and fills the bathroom in fog. It chips away at the cold under my skin that seems to be bone deep. Just as I begin to feel a sliver of relaxation, Max clears his throat and I am reminded of his presence. Images of him throwing open the shower curtain, stabbing furiously, tearing my flesh from bone viciously, enter my mind and that tiny bit of peace I clung to moments ago is instantly gone.

I peer through the small opening in the shower curtain and see Max standing at the sink, his reflection showing his facial stubble disappearing as he runs the razor up his cheek.

After my shower, I stand at the double sink beside Max, doing my hair and makeup. He smiles at me as I glance at him in the reflection. I return the gesture, but never put down my guard.

Breakfast is uneventful and filled with polite conversation and stretches of silence.

I wash the breakfast dishes and wait for my goodbye kiss on the cheek, then listen to the mudroom door close behind Max. I mimic my stalking tendencies from yesterday, minus nearly running over my own mailbox, and follow Max all the way to Billy's office. He may be plotting my murder, but he apparently cares to ensure Billy's life continues as normal.

I consider waiting it out in the parking lot to see if he leaves again, or try to search the SUV again, but suddenly remember that I need to make favor cupcakes for delivery tomorrow morning. At least it will give me something to do that I actually enjoy. Hopefully, I can let my mind rest enough to take a quick nap while I am alone and safe in the house.

Chapter Twenty-Eight

The following morning, Max again plays the perfect little imposter and goes to Billy's job. I watch him cross the parking lot and enter the office building before I continue my journey to the run-down gas station in the middle of nowhere.

When I arrive, I check the cake boxes holding the four dozen cupcakes for the umpteenth time and am pleased to see them completely undamaged by the drive. I have always been proud of my baking. *A good wife keeps her husband's stomach full and his dick wet, Katherine.* My Mama's advice to her teenage daughter. The same Mama that gave weekly lectures about virginity and that no man wants a *dirty bird.*

For Mama, baking was just another necessary life skill for any girl. Something that needs to be ingrained young. For me, baking became a rare joy in my life. A way to receive praise, a way to exert control over something. I would have baked constantly growing up, but Mama warned me I was becoming too fat to get a husband. I had gained two pounds that month. More likely water weight than a few too many muffins and pies.

The clock on the car's dashboard shines just after nine in the morning, and I check my phone for any unread messages, finding nothing. A time had never been set for our meet up, and I would honestly prefer the least amount of documented contact as possible. I would rather wait around with no end time in mind than text that man again.

The wait isn't long, and within minutes I see him walking out of a shadow near the hedges that line the parking lot. I wonder what is actually behind this lot. He clearly knows.

"Hey." I say as I exit my car, walking toward the passenger door to gather the goodies.

"I wasn't sure you would show."

"Why wouldn't I?"

"You laughed in my face, like it was some joke."

"I mean, it just wasn't the favor I was expecting. I still think you might be pranking me or something."

"No prank."

"Okay. Well, I made four dozen, each a different flavor. You've got Black Forest chocolate, blueberry cheesecake, strawberry lemonade, and churro." I lift the four disposable cake boxes from my passenger seat and hand them to the man who traded hemlock for cupcakes.

"Damn, these are serious. Making me look like I went to some fancy bakery."

I smile. A sense of pride floods me. "Thanks! They will taste just as good as they look, promise. I may have thought you were messing with me, but I take my baking very seriously."

"Your husband must have been a damn fool not appreciating this."

His words leave me momentarily speechless. Why is he bringing that up again?

"I guess so." I answer curtly.

"My kid's gunna be happy."

"These are for your kid?" My icy tone instantly melts.

"It's my kid's birthday. She wants cupcakes at school. You just made me a hero for the day."

I laugh. "The request makes much more sense now. I'm happy to help, any time."

"I might take you up on that offer."

"As long as it's just cupcakes, you can call on that favor any time."

He laughs and I feel my view of this man changing. The atmosphere he chooses to hang around in, the speed in which he was willing to help a woman in need of getting rid of her husband…I just assumed he must be pretty scummy. Somehow, being a decent dad shatters that view. He is human just like the rest of us.

Chapter Twenty-Nine

As I drive back toward town, I decide to stop at Billy's office, since it is nearing lunch time. I park between two large trucks, near the back of the lot, five rows away from Billy's car.

Flipping down the mirror, I touch up my lipstick and open my compact, powdering away the shine on my nose. No amount of makeup can hide the tired look of my skin today. I flip a rouge curl away from my face and readjust the clip pinning back the left side of my hair. What a mess I am today, Mama is probably turning in her grave.

I think back to the day she passed. That same bout of guilt appears immediately and the familiar nausea starts. Daddy had already been gone for four years. Mama's passing should have hit me harder than it did, but I barely grieved. I just felt relief. It was the beginning of my life changing. It was the first time I considered what my life had become, and who had led me to this dead-end pit. She led me there, then left me to rot in that pit all alone, trapped like an animal, completely reliant on Billy. Did she really think she did what was best for me? I often wonder if she just didn't know any better.

Thirty minutes of overthinking later, Max walks across the parking lot toward Billy's car. I wiggle in my seat, excitement that my waiting is over buzzes through me. Another man exits the office building, jogging to catch up to the Imposter, a drift of deep voices floating toward me. They are too far away to hear what the conversation entails, but I assume they are discussing lunch plans. A minute later and Max is waving him off, walking toward Billy's car again, his jaw set in determination.

As he gets in the driver's seat, I sit up a bit, readying myself to follow him to whatever restaurant he is heading to. I get lucky, the man who stopped Max for a brief conversation pulls his truck directly behind Billy's SUV as they wait to exit the parking lot. This gives me enough buffer to feel confident that I will not be seen.

A minute passes and both vehicles are pulling out of the parking lot, heading in the same direction. If they were going to the same place, wouldn't they have taken only one car? I follow behind the truck, appreciative of its ability to hide my sedan from view. I slow as we approach a traffic light and allow the yellow to turn, forcing me to stop for the red. I watch the two cars leaving me behind, a straight road ahead that allows me to continue watching from a distance.

I silently pat myself on the back for the decision as I watch the truck behind Max turn into a plaza, and Max continue driving straight. So, they aren't eating together. Then where is Max going?

The light turns green and I follow Max from a comfortable distance. He soon turns right into a shopping plaza and parks. I have no choice but to continue driving for a few minutes, and U-turning first chance I get. Pulling into the plaza while he is parking would be too risky.

As I find a parking spot of my own a few minutes later, I glance toward Billy's Tahoe and see that it is empty. I exhale deeply, feeling a sense of relief as I choose a parking spot that is hidden enough, while still providing a view of the SUV. I can't chance getting out of the car yet, since I have no idea where Max is.

I look around the plaza, realizing that we are in front of the swanky restaurant, The Tortoiseshell Table. This is the place I had begged Billy to take me to, only to be continuously disappointed. Apparently, we didn't need to pay for meals since it was my job to cook them at home. That's what I get for being a good cook, I guess. Or maybe I was just married to a sorry excuse of a man.

Why would Max go here for his lunch break? Seems silly to spend so much money on a rushed meal. Maybe the real Max is fancier than I realize. I again flip down the mirror and check my reflection, quickly touching up my lipstick and powder. I may be a newfound stalker, but I still want to look good. You just never know when you will need to look your best, so you might as well never be caught looking your worst.

The front door of the drugstore next door to The Tortoiseshell Table swings open and Max exits the building, a small plastic shopping bag swinging from his hand. He drove past numerous drugstores closer to Billy's office, why chose here specifically? The bag is tiny, but who knows with this man. He probably forgot something for his murder kit and found out this is the only drugstore with no security cameras or something.

Instead of walking toward the parking lot, Max turns right and enters the coveted restaurant next door. Okay, so he *is* throwing money at an overpriced but definitely delicious lunch. A pang of jealousy hits me and I grunt in annoyance. Even *this* husband would rather eat at a fancy restaurant without me.

Just as I begin to think a closer view is needed, the door to the restaurant opens again and Max exits. What is he doing? No one eats a meal in under ten minutes and there are no to go bags in his hands. Maybe he just had a quick drink at the bar. A little midday pick-me-up.

Instead of walking back to the car, Max stands to the left side of the front door, glancing around anxiously. He must be waiting for someone. Great. Even my imposter husband is cheating on me, and doing it at the same restaurant as my real husband.

He begins to pace near the side of the building, the tiny drugstore bag now balled up, gripped tightly in his left hand. His lips are moving, as if talking to himself. I have never seen the Imposter look so anxious.

A moment later, the door to The Tortoiseshell Table swings open wildly and a petite blonde leaves the restaurant. Her sky-high gold stilettos, endlessly long tan legs, skin tight little black dress and long blonde hair swinging along her waistline, all make their way toward Max. Wow, she's gorgeous. Okay, I get it, Imposter.

She approaches him confidently, playing with her hair as they talk. Despite this complete smoke show gracing Max with her presence, he doesn't seem to notice her beauty at all. His eyes never linger, and his expression seems serious, if not a bit annoyed.

He leans toward her, handing her something that I am unable to see from this distance. She then examines her hand, unfolding a dollar bill of unknown denomination, and studying it for a moment, as if to ensure it isn't counterfeit. Why is Max handing her money? I begin feeling a bit uncomfortable at the thought that I may be watching something I am not supposed to see. Is Max hiring a high-class escort on his lunch break?

The lovely woman slides the money into her bra, easily accessible by the low neckline of her dress, and begins chatting to Max again. They remain in conversation for no more than ten minutes before she goes back into the restaurant, leaving Max staring at his own feet. He kicks at the ground softly; his hands balled into fists by his side. I watch his shoulders sag as he begins to walk back to the car, his jaw tight and eyes like slits. He is clearly deep in thought, and whatever is in that brain of his, doesn't seem pleasant.

Chapter Thirty

The following day I tail Max to work and realize I am getting pretty good at this whole stalking thing. I am beginning to find fun in it, and relish in the adrenaline that surges through me as I avoid being discovered.

On the other hand, the hours of waiting for something to happen take their toll on me, my mind wandering to all the things I have worked so hard to lock away for good.

When Billy was alive, I spent so much time being lonely. The whole world turned around me, I smiled and said all the right things, but I allowed the real me to crumble inside myself until she was nothing but ashes. I became the façade I portrayed. I realize now that I too, am an imposter. I guess there are two of us who can go by that title.

There is no reason that I should be any less lonely than I have always been, but I am. The Imposter has given me a new meaning in a once meaningless life. Answers to chase, truths that I am now forced to accept. Somehow, I am more company than I have ever been.

Sometimes, I catch myself daydreaming about what I will do with my newfound freedom. This is the first time I have ever asked myself what I want out of my life. What career would I want? Do I ever want children? Would I ever want to marry again, or am I better off single?

This, of course, raises the question…where does this end with the Imposter? He is not unpleasant. Perhaps I would have never wanted to kill Billy, had the Imposter been in his place all along. But that is not reality. Billy is dead, and Max is an imposter who decided to take his place. I sigh.

I have spent my entire life on the path already laid before me. A path that is perfectly paved, lined with beautiful daisies, and incredibly easy on my unsure feet.

When I finally wandered, choosing the rough terrain beneath my feet instead, in hopes for a path better suited than my own, that too was taken from me. Max stepped directly in front of me, guiding me back to the perfect pavement, like a lost child. An irrational anger builds inside me.

First, it was Mama.

Next, it was Billy.

Now, it is Max.

I am yet to figure out what the Imposter's end goal is. Nevertheless, I have decided on my own.

I will walk my own path…without any husband.

There my Mama goes, turning over again.

Chapter Thirty-One

Thursday starts like every day, minus the bullshit affirmations that I am convinced do nothing for me. I continue playing the perfect wife role, ensuring Max leaves the house with a full stomach. I swear, I will never cook again once I am on my own.

The morning's stalking session brings nothing of interest, and I find myself leaving the office parking lot and driving toward the run-down gas station where the cupcake loving stranger seems to spend all his time. I don't know why I am drawn here…inviting would be the very last thing this building could be accused of.

The realization of my loneliness has forced me to look at each of the relationships in my life. This stranger, the man who offered to dispose of my husband's now rotting corpse, is the only person in this world who knows what I have done. Well, besides the Imposter. Though, I can't exactly talk about it with the Imposter, can I?

I park my car in the same spot I always find myself in and get out, sitting on the curb. I have no plans to meet my stranger friend, so I have no expectations of seeing him here.

Instead, I find comfort in the place where I can be completely myself. No ginormous secret. No mask of unrealistic perfection. Just a woman in a swing dress and heels, who could never look more out of place, in this place that feels like it is exactly where I belong.

I would question who I have become, but I'm not convinced I even knew who I was before.

The warm late morning sun beats down on my face and I close my eyes, basking in this peaceful moment. I let my mind rest, the worries slowly melting in the heat now finding its way under my skin.

"Surprised to see you here."

I jump, my eyelids opening so swiftly, I feel the flutter of my mascara coated lashes against the tender skin under my eyebrows. I nearly jump to my feet, suddenly fearing for my safety in a place like this, but he begins sitting beside me before I can even try to get to my feet.

"I could say the same to you." I mutter, closing my eyes to cling to one more peaceful moment.

"I don't think it would make as much sense. My whole existence revolves around this place to you. I could live here, in that bush, for all you know."

"How very specific, pointing to that bush. I'm now starting to question if you really do live there."

"It's prime real estate."

"Well, don't be rude. Show me around, then."

We smile at our banter and I feel the same warmth blooming in my chest that I felt at the thought of his daughter. Is this man an actual friend? Perhaps my only friend. I don't even know his name and I am calling him my only real friend. Have I always been this pathetic?

"Is everything okay?" He asks, an undertone of actual worry in his voice.

"As okay as it can be, I guess."

"My offer still stands."

"He's already dead." My frank admission surprises me. I have held the words inside, only daring to silently speak them inside my own head. I imagined a deep chasm of worry opening if they ever left my lips, but instead I feel a light buzzing in my head. An entirely pleasant dizziness passes through me and I suddenly feel lighter.

"I know. I meant with disposal." He replies, completely unfazed by my admission. He sounds so matter of fact. Is it the distance he has from the death or is he so well versed in murder that it feels like discussing the weather?

"Oh. I mean…eventually, yes, I will need to figure something out. I'm not entirely comfortable with his current placement."

"The longer you wait, the worse it will be. Especially if he is outside. Trust me."

"He is outside, so, yeah. I will figure something else out soon."

My mind has been elsewhere. The Imposter has been quite the distraction. I admit, I have completely forgotten that I am supposed to be figuring out what to do with Billy's body long term. Once the Imposter is gone, the police will eventually have to become involved in Billy's sudden disappearance.

I can't have his body anywhere near the house, or anywhere I visit, really. I have grown to trust this stranger more than anyone else in my life, not that it means much. Do I trust him enough to get rid of a body for me? There is no going back from that. There is no talking my way around that. He will become complicit. Am I ready to put myself at the mercy of someone else in that way?

"Is he in the woods behind your house?"

My head whips around, eyes burning a hole into the side of this stranger's scarred face. "How would you know that?"

He laughs. "It was a guess. Where else would a housewife hide a body? I assume he is at least twice your weight. It's not exactly an easy task."

"It's not an easy task, but it's a task I figured out on my own. I will figure out the rest, too."

"Suit yourself. You know where to find me if you change your mind."

"Yeah." I point toward the bush he always appears from. "In your house."

"You sound jealous."

"Maybe a tiny bit."

"You need to move him. That's the kind of stupid mistake that gets you caught." His tone has become serious, voice hushed even though no one is around us.

"Why are you helping me?" I blurt before I can stop myself.

He stares at me for a moment, the darkness in his eyes seem to beckon me to climb inside. An irrational feeling, willing you to get lost in the endless black. Somehow terrifying and comforting at the same time.

"My sister's boyfriend was a real piece of shit. She wouldn't listen…thought she could handle it. She's dead now. It should be him buried in the woods behind the house. Instead, it was my sister."

"I'm so sorry, I didn't mean to bring something so terrible up."

"There's no bringing it up. It's always there, it never leaves."

"Sorry." I whisper.

"Any man who hurts a woman deserves to die. You gave me that revenge in your own way, don't say sorry."

"He never hurt me like that. Not physically, at least."

"He was not a good man."

"That's true." The confirmation from someone else's lips instantly quiets the constant questioning in my head.

"It is a small man that harms the innocent. No changing men like that. Death is their fate…and for many, it is more merciful than they deserve."

"That's pretty profound."

"Grief gives you endless time to think."

We both remain silent, staring into the vast lot of concrete and asphalt, lost in the thoughts brought on by our own versions of the monster called grief.

Chapter Thirty-Two

The comfortable silence surrounding our concrete bubble is popped as the text tone screams from my phone. I rummage through my pocketbook, wondering for the umpteenth time how anything can get lost inside such a small pouch. When I finally locate the largest item in the bag, I see Lucy's name on the screen.

"Should I bring anything tonight?"

I open the message and begin typing, giving letters to my confusion, before I suddenly recall that it is Thursday. My women's bible study group. Last Thursday's bake sale coupled with questioning who the hell is sleeping beside me each night has thrown me off schedule.

I leap to my feet, smoothing my dress while explaining to the nameless stranger who has become my nameless friend that I need to go. I pull out of the parking lot quickly, my tires emitting a soft squeal, giving away my haste.

As I pull into the driveway, I quickly text Lucy back, letting her know that she only needs to bring herself. I rush inside and begin my work in the kitchen, ensuring that nothing appears rushed or forgotten. I may not have any true friends, but this group of church goers has seen me twice a week since I was old enough to host the bible study. They will sense if anything is off.

A few hours later, the kitchen island presents a spread of sandwiches, pastries, cookies, and large jugs of sweet tea. A circle of chairs fills the living room; a worn and well-loved bible placed on each of the seat cushions. I place a patchwork knit blanket gently on one of the chairs, knowing Ms. Josephine tends to get cold. While I cannot genuinely call this group my friends, I do care deeply for each of them. It is not lost on me that my façade has prevented me from true friendships. Somehow it always seemed more important what others thought about me, then how they felt about me.

Twenty minutes before the group is scheduled to arrive, I decide to freshen up in the bedroom. *There is never a reason not to look your best.* I am trying to find myself away from the people who have controlled my life, but some things are so engrained, it is just second nature. I fluff my curls in the mirror, tighten the backs of my earrings and search the bathroom countertop for a gold bangle that would look lovely with this dress. The search proves fruitless, so I walk to the vanity in the bedroom, knowing it must be in my jewelry box.

As I approach, I see a small gold lipstick tube in the center of the vanity, balanced upright like a little soldier, standing at attention. How did that get there? I don't remember leaving out one of my lipsticks. I turn the tube in my hand, opening the cap and twisting up the pigmented wax to reveal an untouched but familiar color. *Toast of New York*. The lipstick I claimed to have lost, pretending to search my car floor so I could spy on Max when I only knew him as the Imposter.

He bought me a lipstick.

The correct lipstick.

A warm feeling spreads through my middle and my eyes prickle with emotion. Am I really tearing up over a lipstick? I sigh. The gesture feels so touching, so romantic, and I am again reminded that Billy was an ass. He never showed small gestures of care. Why is the Imposter treating me this way? Does he truly want to take the place of Billy for good? It almost feels like a different version of Billy, trying to make up for all the mistakes, all the years of cold I have lived in.

The man buys me a lipstick…but what about the murder kit? It is possible that all of the small acts of kindness are just a way of ensuring my guard is down? I want to believe that I have it all wrong. I want Max to be good, but my past has taught me that is rarely the case. It has taught me to never trust. The face we see is too often nothing more than a mask.

The echo of a shrill tune fills my home and I recap the lipstick, shoving it into the drawer of the vanity. I check the mirror, plastering a smile on my face, then stride to the front door to welcome the waiting group inside.

Chapter Thirty-Three

Forty minutes later, the bible study group sits in the circle of chairs, plates of goodies balanced on their laps. Our meetings typically last two to three hours, depending on how good the weekly gossip is. When Billy was alive, he did his best to avoid the house during my bible study meetings. *You think God doesn't notice your bible study is more of a neighborhood smear campaign than an act of faith?* He was always questioning my faith, as if it is something that fits into a simple box.

Max has yet to arrive home and I begin to wonder if he has taken a cue from Billy, and found something better to do than socialize with these ladies. In this moment, I don't blame him. I am finding it hard to focus on the chatter of the group, and spend far too much time staring out the window, wondering what the Imposter is up to.

"Did y'all hear about Sarah and George?" The plump brunette twirls her fingers through her shoulder length bob, a rather pleased look on her round face as she glances to each of the women.

"Do tell, Maryanne." The sly response leaving the thin, burgundy-colored lips belonging to the woman seated to Maryanne's right.

"Well, I heard that they are discussing an open marriage situation, can you imagine?" Maryanne relishes in her words, sipping her iced tea and smirking at the gasping responses. She lives for this weekly moment. I can only imagine how boring her marriage must be.

I smooth the skirt of my dress as I stand from my seat, walking the circle, offering to take any finished plates. A pile of used dishware in hand, I stride to the kitchen, wanting to get away from the gossip that seems so tiny in the currently vast world inside my own head. I take my time washing the dishes, not worrying in the slightest about my hostess duties.

Once I have tidied the kitchen and hidden away as long as possible, I reenter the living room, jug of sweet tea in hand.

"Can I top y'all off?" I ask, plastering that plastic smile on my face once again.

A few of the ladies utter affirmative responses, and I do a counterclockwise walk through the circle, refilling glasses. The chatter continues to fill the room, and a buzzing in my ears seems to drown it out, making it impossible to focus on the words. When I am again seated in the circle, I hear the mudroom door open and close. The Imposter is home.

His approaching footsteps echo above the chatter and buzzing in my ears, sounding like the beat of a snare drum. No one else seems to notice the approach.

"Hey there, ladies." The Imposter states, a warmth as thick as honey dripping from his voice.

Each of the women turn, excitedly greeting the man they believe to be my husband. Obvious surprise on some of the faces, considering this will be Billy's first appearance to bible study in twelve years.

My legs suddenly operate of their own accord, and I pop up from my seat, skittering toward Max. I lean in and kiss his lips sweetly, my voice chipper as I greet the man these ladies believe I have been in love with since my teens. “Hey Sugar, surprised to see you home so early.”

He recovers quickly from the surprise of my sudden affection, and to his credit, he picks up quickly on the façade that is deeply engrained in me. “Well, I can’t stay long, but I just wanted to pop by and give my beautiful wife a kiss.”

The women all coo their praise, stroking Max’s ego with their comments about what a wonderful husband he must be. *If only they knew, he isn’t my husband at all.*

“Katherine is just so very sweet, bless her heart, I am sure she makes it too easy to be married to her.” Maryanne comments, the corners of her lips curling up in a way that makes it feel like a dig. I know her well enough to assume she is implying that I am a pushover.

Before I can respond, Max’s voice fills the room. “Don’t be fooled now, she’s like whiskey in a tea cup. Lucky for me, whiskey is my favorite drink.”

The smile on Maryanne’s lips falls, and for the first time in possibly all of her existence, she is at a loss for words. She is likely realizing this is the first time she has seen Billy come to my aid in any way. I bet she's wondering how long it has been since her husband said something like that about her.

I kiss Max's cheek, and for the first time in my existence, it is not a show. It is a genuine thank you for treating me as a husband should treat a wife.

He is not my husband.

I am not his wife.

Yet, this façade feels more real than any I have faked before.

Chapter Thirty-Four

"I'll get out of your hair now. Have a nice time, ladies."

With that, Max leaves the room to continue its energetic chatter and I return to my seat, the same plastic smile on my face. It has become so natural around these women, I don't even force my lips to do it, it just happens without my consent. The mudroom door opens and closes, I sigh, feeling suddenly alone in a room full of people.

"Excuse me a moment, ladies." I state, leaving the room quickly to avoid any questions.

I am drawn to the window facing the driveway. I want to watch Max drive away, imagining myself following behind, continuing my search for answers. The jabber of the living room has been softened by the distance and I breathe a sigh of relief for the reprieve my ears receive.

Billy's car still rests in the driveway and I crane my neck to look for Max sitting in the driver's seat. It is empty. Where is he? I glance around me, suddenly paranoid that he is standing behind me. I heard the mudroom door; he must have gone outside.

I wander toward the kitchen, staring through each of the windows I pass. Movement in the back yard catches my eye from the window over the kitchen sink. I slink toward it, unable to take my curious gaze off of Max as he walks toward the shed. My stomach turns, the taste of bile in my mouth, the burn in my throat threatening to send me running to the bathroom.

He has no reason to go to the shed…what is he doing? The sound around me drowns out completely as all of my senses pass their power into my sight. The world around me blacks out and there is nothing but Max, snooping around the evidence of my husband's murder. He bypasses the shed and continues walking, straight into the woods.

Chapter Thirty-Five

The panic is setting in and I can feel a trickle of sweat dripping down my spine. Every primal instinct inside of me is screaming to run after Max, to make sure he doesn't find Billy's body.

I can't leave now; I have a room full of women using the guise of God to gossip about the people they call friends. If I leave now, these women will know something is wrong. Even worse, they may follow me into the woods. At the very least, they may think it would be something worth gossiping about, which means they would *definitely* follow me into those woods.

No. I have no choice. I have to stay and continue to host these buffoons while the Imposter has free rein to look for my husband's body. The moment I feel a small building block of trust being placed, it is used against me. We were just smiling, kissing, acting like a married couple. He knows I am stuck with these women and he is using it to his advantage. *Touche, Imposter.*

A plate of snickerdoodles in hand, I decide to end my torturous position near the window and return to the living room. I offer the sweets to each woman, then return to my seat in the circle.

"Are you okay, Katherine? You look ill, honey." Josephine's tender hand touches my knee.

"Yes, ma'am, I'm doing just fine." The lie takes more effort than I expected. I am sweating like a rich whore in church and I pray this sweet woman believes me.

Her eyes linger for a moment, clearly seeing the heat burning red up my neck. I find it much easier to omit things than flat out lie. Mama especially hated liars. I can hear her icy words like she is sitting beside me. *Pretty is as pretty does, Katherine.*

"Okay, sweetie." Josephine's hand now bounces on my knee, patting me lovingly.

"That husband of yours, does he have family in Bearios?"

I stare into the crystal blue eyes, surrounded by far too much cakey mascara. Her orangey tan skin perfectly unblemished, contrasting aggressively to the ivory white row of veneers. She calls herself Pearl. Her real name is Margaret. I wish I knew neither of those things.

"No, his whole family grew up here in Starfire. All of them have now passed." The most truthful statement I have made in the last few weeks.

"Y'all, I saw the most terrible thing on the news a few weeks ago. Some woman missing from Bearios. They think it was the husband. It's *always* the husband. He looks so much like Billy, just a different nose and hair, really. I thought maybe they were cousins, some kind of kin, at least."

I swallow down the lump now forming in my suddenly parched throat. She is talking about Max. Does she know? I nearly laugh at myself. She doesn't know. There is no way anyone would believe my reality right now. If I told any of these women I killed my husband, then woke up beside an imposter…I would find myself in an inpatient clinic faster than I could pack a bag full of lipstick.

"He's an only child, with no cousins. The only child of a generation for that family. Most of 'em didn't believe in marriage, I suppose."

"That's unusual."

"To each their own."

"Strange coincidence, I guess." Pearl comments.

"Must be." I reply, hoping to squash this line of questioning at the natural break of conversation, I stand again. "Can I get anything from the kitchen? More sweet tea?"

A few of the women nod and I don't wait for any further reason to leave the room. As I grab a second jug of sweet tea off the kitchen island, Max strides out of the woods. He is empty handed and his clothes look clean. Perhaps he just wanted a walk in nature?

A nice relaxing walk to the body of the man he replaced.

Chapter Thirty-Six

Sleep is becoming a rarity for me. The bright white of the ceiling burns my retinas, as I am unable to force my eyelids to stay closed for longer than a blink. The idea of another day of no sleep fills me with dread, but I worry that a sleeping pill would knock me out so hard, I wouldn't wake up in time to prevent my own murder.

I can't stop thinking about Max's walk in the woods. Why in the world would he need to go in those woods? If it had nothing to do with Billy's body, then what exactly was he doing? What irony it would be if he was scouting the area for my future gravesite. *Even in death, I can't escape Billy.*

The conversation with the hemlock man at the gas station suddenly rings through my head. *You need to move him. That's the kind of stupid mistake that gets you caught.* He is right. If the Imposter suddenly disappears, I will have to report Billy missing. I can't imagine I will have the luxury of a placeholder forever. The first place the police will look is at home, both literally and figuratively.

There is too much liability keeping that pile of rotting flesh anywhere near this house. It can't be anywhere near my life, really. I have to dispose of it somehow. It has to be gone from this earth entirely. Nothing to ever tie me to this crime. I should have taken up Mr. Hemlock on his offer. What do I know about disposing of a body?

Nothing.

Yet, it has to get done. Max may already have the evidence against me to keep me wasting away in a prison cell for the rest of my life. What if he goes to the police? He could anonymously report something that leads right to the body, couldn't he? That would allow him to walk away from all of this like he was never even here.

He won't.

I am sure of that…at least not yet. It is not trust that convinces me to believe that instinct. It is the surety that his undertaking here is not complete. He has not met his end goal. I may not be sure of what exactly that is yet, but I know two things.

His work here is not done.

I need to move the body.

Chapter Thirty-Seven

After following Max to Billy's office on Friday morning, I immediately return home and begin my trek through the woods. Every time I enter these woods, I promise myself it is the last time. So many broken promises, they all just keep piling up. Today, I plan on keeping that promise to myself. This is the last time either of us will be in these woods.

I drag the sled behind me, a shovel and box of large black trash bags tucked inside. I would have preferred to do this in the cover of darkness, but Max's infiltration of these woods has made me feel rushed. I will not sleep until I know this is taken care of. The body rotting away in this hole has left me a sitting duck if the police suddenly come sniffing around, and I refuse to let

Billy take anything else from me. I haven't even tasted my newfound freedom yet, but I actually believe if anyone could take it from me, it would be Billy. Even in death.

I am safer to do it while Max is at work. There is very little concern that a neighbor or passerby would see me, considering these woods are on private property, my property. The Imposter has become the only threat. I don't know what his motive here is, but the two options seem to be killing me or tattling to the authorities. Neither of those options work for me.

I toy with the idea of killing the Imposter. It wouldn't be ideal, just another body to dispose of. If getting rid of Billy's body isn't enough, that will be my only other option. I will do anything to protect my freedom. I am so close to it, for the first time in my life. I can't let it slip away.

The heels of my shoes dig into the dirt slightly as I walk, slowing me down to a totter. In my rush to get out here, I totally forgot to put on my pair of flats. A pair of sneakers sure would come in handy in a situation like this. I owned a pair of sneakers once, for about an hour, before Mama tossed them in the firepit. *You can't make a silk purse out of a sow's ear, Katherine.* I guess I never had a reason to buy another pair after watching my first pair burn, though this is starting to feel like the perfect reason.

The journey takes nearly twice as long as it would in flats, but my determination never wavers. Time is on my side at the moment, as long as I get everything taken care of before Max gets home from work.

Finally, I reach the disturbed pile of dirt encasing my former husband and drop the handle of the sled to the ground. I rub my palms together in an attempt to ease the rope burn now forming between my thumb and index finger. Cursing myself for forgetting gloves, I resign myself to the work ahead of me, sure it will destroy my manicure.

The shovel pierces the ground, the work less difficult than I had expected. The dirt is still soft and fresh, not yet settled back to the hard mound it once was. As the mound becomes smaller, the abrasion on my hand becomes deeper, growing red hot. *Please Lord, forgive me for the things I have done. Forgive me for the things I am about to do.* The pain becomes almost pleasant, a manifestation of what I deserve in some way. The mound of upturned dirt grows larger behind my back and I begin to question the depth of this grave. The adrenaline on the night of my crime must have stolen the reality of time.

How deep is this dang hole? I wipe the sweat trickling down my forehead with the back of my forearm. The white of my swing dress is littered with particles of dirt and it seems almost fitting against the floral pattern. The head of the shovel strikes hard dirt and I groan at the unexpected reverberation going up my arms.

Why is the dirt suddenly so hard? I drop down to my knees and begin sweeping away loose dirt with my hands. There is nothing but a fresh, untouched layer of dirt, several maggots still suckling at the hard, tainted earth.

Billy's body is gone.

Chapter Thirty-Eight

My heart pounds against my ribcage, trying to escape from my chest cavity and I can't seem to steady my breath. This can't be real. *Where the hell is Billy*?

After putting away the sled, shovel and trash bags, I rush inside to change and clean up. I try to convince myself to remain calm, to lose myself in routine and take my mind off of the fact that my dead husband's body is suddenly missing. I cannot.

Instead, I drive to Billy's office. Staying home is making me feel helpless. I have no idea what sitting in the office parking lot is doing for me, but it seems better than nothing. At least I can pretend I am trying to find answers instead of panicking that police are about to knock on my door any minute. I scroll through news apps on my phone, looking for anything announcing a body being found.

Nothing.

In a town like this, a body in an unmarked grave would be headline news for sure.

I clutch my chest, forcing myself to focus on my breathing. I think I am about to have an anxiety attack. I need to slow my heart rate. I need to focus on my breathing. I repeat words designed to calm me inside my head, over and over.

The police are not after you.

They did not find Billy's body.

The news would be all over that.

There is no way they found him.

Look at me, doing affirmations. Lucy would be proud.

It's so hard to believe the voice inside my head. The body did not just disappear, that much is clear. I can't disregard the fact that Max was in those woods yesterday. That must mean something…but I saw him leave shortly after he went in. He had no dirt on his clothes. He had no decomposing body in tow. Is it possible he went back in without me knowing?

Suddenly, movement in the parking lot catches my attention and I see Max hurriedly getting into Billy's car. I glance at the dashboard clock and register that he is leaving work two hours early. Is this a late lunch or is he actually ending his work day? I quietly praise myself for following my instinct in coming here.

Something is going on, and I get the feeling the answers are closer than ever.

Chapter Thirty-Nine

Max pulls the SUV into Uncle Ted's driveway and I watch the car disappear from view behind the overgrown landscape. I pull over to the side of the road and consider my options. I can't just pull into the driveway, and there is nowhere to park where my car wouldn't be seen. As much as I want to see what he is doing, I don't think it is worth risking being spotted.

In this moment, I decide I have to act, but I have to be smart. This man is dangerous. If following him has taught me anything, it is that he is prepared for murder and to cover up the subsequent body. He has taken over my husband's life and I am the only loose end to tie up. Once I am gone, he can continue on as Billy and no one would be the wiser. He must have gotten rid of Billy's body…and mine will be next.

What if he knows I am following him? Perhaps this is a trap. He is waiting patiently for my curiosity to get the better of me. I shudder at the thought.

No, I will not play right into his hand.

As I drive home to prepare dinner, I decide that I will not wait any longer. I will not be a sitting duck.

Tonight, I will act.

Chapter Forty

Max sleeps peacefully beside me, snoring loudly and dribbling drool onto the pillow. I slide out of the bed softly, barely moving the blanket we share. Tiptoeing to his side of the bed, I squeeze the pockets of the pants now thrown onto the floor haphazardly. The key ring slides easily from his pocket. I leave it laying on the pants, refusing to lift it, in case the keys dare to clack together nosily.

After a few tense minutes, and two chipped fingernails later, I manage to remove the four keys that are unfamiliar to me. It must be one of these four. Max's snores continue uninterrupted as I sneak out of the bedroom, padding down the stairs quietly.

I slide into the downstairs bathroom and open the vanity, pulling out a tote bag I stuffed inside earlier today. I quickly change into the clothes folded inside and shove the four loose keys into the pocket of the only pair of jeans I own. I slide my feet into my waiting flats in the mudroom and leave the house quietly.

The drive to Uncle Ted's house goes quick, as there are no other cars on the road and I break the speed limit…only slightly. My eyes dart around the road, searching for police cars while I press down on the gas pedal. I want to press it all the way to the floor, but the last thing I need right now is an interaction with a police officer. Documentation of being out this late will seem extra suspicious if they start getting anonymous tips about my dead husband.

I feel nervous and jittery, unsure what I am about to find as I pull into the driveway. I silently praise the overgrowth now hiding my car from view. As I scurry up the walkway, I remove all four keys from my pocket and begin trying the front door lock. The minutes pass, seemingly endless, until the fourth key finally turns the lock with a satisfying click.

The door creaks as it swings open and I step inside gingerly, suddenly feeling very alone.

"Hello?" I call out.

While I know it is irrational, I feel like I am intruding on Uncle Ted's home. I almost expect to hear him respond.

No one does.

The kitchen light switch clicks on underneath my finger, and I hear a slight buzzing while the bulb seems to warm up. I begin wandering around the home, a light layer of dust coating many of the rooms that have remained untouched for the better half of a decade.

The master bedroom seems so out of place, with its updated bedding and dust free surfaces. As I enter the room, I see a half roll of duct tape sitting on the dresser top. I approach the wooden surface, bringing the floor hidden by the right side of the bed into view. A clear plastic bag appears to have been thrown erratically toward the floor, partially caught onto the handle of the nightstand.

I pick up the empty bag and see the label announcing its contents as a large blue tarp. I drop the bag and begin to back up, suddenly needing distance from whatever is happening inside this room. As I walk backwards, I trip over something laying on the floor near the underside of the bed, my back hitting the dresser and stopping my fall. I glance at the offending object and see a pair of women's shoes now spread wildly across the floor.

Those are not my shoes.

Uncle Ted never married.

Why is there a pair of women's shoes here? Why is there used duct tape here? Where is the tarp that once called that plastic bag home?

A wave of panic begins to overwhelm me as questions flash through my mind at a rapid pace, and I am forced to accept that something is very, very wrong. I want to look away. I want to run out of this house and get to the safety of my car.

I cannot look away.

My eyes are glued to the lovely little dark red kitten heels now burning a hole in my mind. Mentally, I cannot leave this room. Physically, my body is choosing flight, continuing to back out slowly.

Until my body slams into someone.

I whip around and see Max standing in the doorway, watching me become witness to whatever crimes he has committed in this room. I glance down to the black gloves covering his hands. My legs immediately begin creating distance, forcing me further inside the room again.

"Katherine. What are you doing here?"

"I should be asking you that, Max!"

The Imposter pauses, the surprise impossible to hide. "You know who I am?"

"You killed your wife, didn't you? Did you dispose of her here? You killed her, Max!" My voice raises with each word, the panic inside me forcing its way out.

"I didn't kill my wife."

The sorrow in his voice is heartbreaking. He stares into my eyes and I see tears beginning to form as his lips create the words that ring in my ears.

"Billy did."

PART TWO

The Imposter

Chapter Forty-One

The Imposter

One Year Ago

Marnie is cheating on me; I just know it.

At first, I thought this was just grief manifesting in strange ways that I didn't understand. It's a feeling deep in my gut that I just can't shake. It whispers in my ear constantly, wrapping around my brain tightly and squeezing until I can no longer ignore it. I have started to question if I am going crazy.

We have always been so happy together, I never imagined I would have to worry about something like this.

Two months ago, Marnie's mother passed away in a botched surgery, and it absolutely destroyed her. It destroyed us all, really. Death is never easy, but when it is unexpected, the hole it rips open somehow feels more violent.

I didn't blame her when she pulled away from me.

I didn't blame her for acting distant.

Grief does strange things, and I just thought this was part of her process. Who am I to tell her what she needs right now? I just wish *she* would tell me what she needs. I would give that girl the entire world if I had it in my hands. Meanwhile, I don't need nothin' but her.

That dang itch keeps nagging just under the skin and I can't ignore it any longer. If I don't just quiet these nagging voices, quiet this *feeling*, then I actually will lose my mind soon. I feel terrible for even thinking any of this, but I have to ease my own overactive mind. I'm sure Marnie would feel the same way if roles were reversed. I'm sure she would understand my suspicions.

Marnie leaves for work and I decide to follow her, just to quiet myself.

Just to be sure.

She stops by her brother's house to drop off the meals she made for him, like she has every week since their mother passed. She has always been the glue. That one family member who is completely selfless, always choosing the well-being of everyone else. She never utters a complaint about the late nights making extra food, or the early wake ups to make sure she could go check on Nikolas. Hell, she even cleans his house on her days off. I know she worries about him. I worry about her.

I wait patiently, parked in a nearby lot outside of Nikolas' neighborhood, expecting to see Marnie's car leaving the neighborhood, turning left toward work. Ten minutes pass and I watch as the familiar little red sedan approaches the stop sign, then turns right out of the neighborhood.

Why would she be turning away from work?

My stomach clenches violently underneath my flannel shirt and I fight the terrible things my mind is telling me.

Please don't let my intuition be true.

Please don't shatter me, Marnie.

I follow Marnie to a restaurant near the outskirts of town and watch her approach a man waiting outside.

They kiss.

I break completely.

Chapter Forty-Two

Nine Months Ago

It is hard to admit that I am becoming obsessed.

I know I shouldn't do it, but I find myself following Marnie every day now. It started with just every once in a while, one trip every few days. I didn't really need to know what she was doing, I had already gotten the worst answer to every question I had imagined.

After the first two weeks of those answers stewing in my brain, I started to come up with new questions. Questions that could only be answered by following Marnie again. Questions that I should never ask of my own wife, and answers that should never have found their way to any husband.

She meets with him nearly every day. I follow them to restaurants, his office building and even a house that must belong to him. The landscaping is so overgrown, he should be ashamed to bring a woman over…especially a woman as wonderful as Marnie.

At first, I thought she had trapped herself inside this bubble of grief and began to feel so lonely, that she stepped out of our marriage. I assumed she would snap out of it quickly, find herself filled with regret at her indiscretions. I am wholeheartedly prepared to forgive her the moment it happens. I dream of that moment every day. Everything out in the open, everything forgiven, and our marriage free of pain and secrets, like it had been for so long.

This pain is unbearable. Is she confiding the pain of her grief in this man instead of me? How can this stranger, this person she has known for mere months, take the place of me? I want to be her shoulder to cry on. I want to be her strength when she is weak. I want to be everything we vowed to be in this marriage.

What does he have that I do not? I admit that physically, we are very similar. Sure, his nose is much straighter than mine, likely never having it broken in fights of his younger days, like I had. I thought Marnie liked the rugged look it gave me. She certainly didn't mind when we met.

His hair is darker than mine, but I thought Marnie preferred light hair. I often thought my light brown, nearly sandy blonde, was even too dark for her taste. The man's eyebrows somehow seem cleaner than mine, less wiry and wild. That's something that is easily fixed, right? I find myself nitpicking everything about him, comparing his every physical trait to my own. Is it as simple as sexual attraction?

Sure, our physical relationship has changed over the years, but I still find it entirely satisfying. I have never desired another woman since the moment I laid eyes on Marnie. Is she not as satisfied as she has claimed? Have I become too selfish to notice her unhappiness?

I softly move the branch scratching my right arm, careful to readjust it silently. I return my gaze to the small hole in the bedroom blinds of the house with the overgrown yard, watching this man satisfy the woman I have loved for practically my entire life.

A small bead of sweat drips down the side of his face and I notice that perfect nose yet again. I wonder if he has had a nose job or if God has simply gifted this asshole with perfection.

His eyes gaze down on the naked body of my wife and I scowl at the shit brown color. I have always been complimented on my sea blue eyes. Sure, they aren't those unforgettable crystal blue eyes that everyone raves about, but they aren't *shit brown.*

Maybe Marnie prefers dark eyes. I guess I have never asked her that.

Marnie's pinnacle is reached and I hear her moan the unfamiliar name.

It is poison entering my ears, burying deep inside my brain.

Billy.

Chapter Forty-Three

Six Months Ago

My entire existence has begun to revolve around Marnie and Billy. It has been six months since I first discovered the affair. How long will this go on behind my back before Marnie's guilt sets in? Does she even care that she has destroyed me on a cellular level?

Nikolas pulls his white truck to the front door of the Hartford Plastic Surgery Center and the nurse assists me out of the wheelchair. I climb into the truck gingerly, wobbling from medication rather than pain. It is a pain I have known before, just in a very different way.

"You look beautiful." Nikolas coos as the nurse closes the passenger door.

"Gee, thanks." I mutter, already dreading any pending prodding questions.

I flip down the mirror and stare at my now warmly lit face. My under eyes are beginning to look slightly bruised, they'll be purple before long. The bandages surrounding my nose push up the tip slightly and I look like a pig. I pray this is far from the end result. Marnie certainly doesn't want a man with a pig nose…probably even less than a man with a boxer's nose.

"I mean that's why you did this, right? You want to look beautiful for my sister. What a lucky girl." Nikolas continues to poke fun as we begin to drive.

My nerves are shot and his comments are particularly grating.

Whether it is the massive amount of pain killers surging through my system, or the pain of hearing my brother in law's good-natured jabs, I find my mood plummeting. I leave the jabs unanswered, focusing my attention out the passenger window instead.

My nose is a stark contrast to Billy's. It was a drastic fix, but it had to be done. Why would I ever think a woman like Marnie would want a nose so crooked?

The bridge basically touched each cheek. It was a mess. It will be perfect now. It will be something my wife can be proud of. Surely, she will find me more attractive now.

Surely, everything will go back to normal.

Chapter Forty-Four

Four Months Ago

The bandages have been off of my nose for a few weeks now and I am incredibly impressed with the results. Not only is my nose now perfect…it looks exactly like Billy's. The similarities in our looks have become much more prominent now. I'm sure this has pleased Marnie.

I remain patient. I know that Marnie has been with Billy for eight months now, probably longer. I can't expect her to immediately break it off with him, now that her husband is becoming more attractive. I do my best to woo her, to win her back. The problem is…there are no real problems between us.

We rarely argue. Our view on life, politics, and religion all align. We don't have that one nagging difference that just keeps coming back to create ripples in our relationship. Everything has always been wonderful, easy even. And she treats me no different than she did before Billy.

If I hadn't seen the affair with my own eyes, more times than I can count, I wouldn't have believed it was happening. Marnie still treats me as though I am her everything. She isn't distant anymore. Yet, she is in a shell. Something is different about *her*, not about us.

She questioned the nose job, acting as if it was unnecessary. She is so sweet to protect my feelings. I played it off with some bullshit about doing it to please myself, ease my own insecurities. Her eyes lingered on my face, seeming to say all the words that her lips wouldn't. Is she thinking of Billy as her eyes search her husband's face? If she hadn't noticed that she has a type, she sees it in that moment.

But still, she confesses nothing.

Chapter Forty-Five

Three Months Ago

Nine months of watching this affair has really taken its toll on me. I refuse to confront you. As much as I want it out in the open, it needs to come from you. How long will I let this go on, if you never confess your sins?

After a brief bout of hanky-panky in the backseat of Billy's SUV, you return to your car and begin freshening up. You remove a hairbrush from your purse and smooth your perfect dark hair. You redo your makeup, surely having worked up a sweat from your little tryst. I watch as you leave the parking lot, likely coming home to me.

Billy leaves behind you, turning the opposite direction than I had expected. I wonder what a man like that needs to do before going home. Maybe he is going to the gym, maybe he cares about things like that.

For the first time in all these months, I decide to follow Billy, instead of you. My curiosity peaks the longer we drive into the town of Starfire. It is a small town, seemingly better off than where I grew up, and I feel the strong sense that I am an outsider. I wonder if Billy grew up here, or if we are just passing through, merely a part of the journey, instead of the destination itself.

The SUV turns into a neighborhood and I continue driving, wanting to create some distance. A few minutes later, I too am inside the neighborhood, searching each driveway for the familiar vehicle my wife sometimes uses as a bedroom.

I finally locate it, parked next to a fancy sedan, beside a massive two-story home. A pang of jealousy twists my guts and I wonder what this home is to Billy. Perhaps another woman he is dating? An irrational anger suddenly clouds me. How dare he cheat on my wife.

The logical side of my brain screams at me to turn around and go home. I should listen; it is the right thing to do. Instead, I search for a spot to park my car that will remain unseen. I continue telling myself to go home as I creep onto the property where Billy's car now rests. I silently agree to give myself ten minutes before I leave, just enough time to give myself some well-deserved answers.

I squeeze into a thick, prickly bush beside a window on the side of the house. While I am confident in the cover this bush gives me, I silently curse the spiky leaves that now rub against every inch of my exposed skin. They simultaneously scratch and burn, pulling at my dark arm hair and making me want to scream. This is a bush from hell.

I peer into the corner of the window, unsure what I am seeing for a few moments, until I realize that I am looking into the dining room. A long wooden table, surrounded by eight tufted back and cushioned chairs, laid so perfectly that it reminds me of those fancy home magazines I have seen in the checkout line at the grocery store.

The beautifully laid table is nothing compared to the angelic woman who walks into the room, setting down a serving tray with a perfectly browned whole chicken atop it.

She is quite beautiful, her curly red hair pinned back on one side, revealing her delicate neck. She wears an emerald green dress, the skirt swinging as she walks, and high heels in the exact same shade of green. It is clear this woman values her looks, and I can't help but to notice that she appears to have just stepped out of the fifties. She remains standing and begins to slice the chicken, serving the food onto the plate in front of the only guest at the table.

Billy watches the woman serving him, a complete lack of emotion on his face. He seems wholly unimpressed and I can't help but feel annoyed for the woman who took the time to make him this meal. After his plate is piled with roast chicken, mashed potatoes and green beans, he lifts his fork and begins eating. The woman in the green dress then begins to serve herself, before finally taking her seat.

He didn't even wait for her before he began eating. I second guess my earlier questioning about this being his hometown…a southern man would have better manners. I grew up dirt poor but was always rich in character. It seems Billy is the reverse of that upbringing.

The woman's chin drops to her chest; her hands laced together in her lap. She is praying before she begins her meal. Clearly, a God fearing, southern woman. What is the relationship between these two? Upon my approach of the home, I thought it must be his family's house. Yet, here are just two people eating a meal. No elderly, or extended family members present.

It dawns on me so suddenly that I feel as if I have been hit by a baseball bat.

Is this lovely woman his wife?

Chapter Forty-Six

Two Months Ago

Every waking moment of the last month has been dedicated to Billy. Both Marnie and I seem to follow this protocol, but she doesn't know that. At first, I wanted to emulate him. I wanted to be the man who kept my wife's attention.

Now, I want him dead.

The last few weeks of watching his every move have proven to me that he is an absolute pig. I once believed that he was a single man, enthralled by the loveliness of my wife, and I couldn't blame him for it. It wasn't his fault for trying, it was my fault for not being good enough to keep her.

That was before I realized he too, is married. Married to an absolutely beautiful woman, who waits on him hand and foot. She looks miserable, and that is understandable. But, so does he. What in the world does he have to be unhappy about? He has two extraordinary women wrapped around his fat finger and he is still a miserable fuck.

I hate him.

I sit in the parking lot of Billy's office, staring at the SUV parked near the front of the lot, under a small tree now blooming white flowers. *I hope a bird shits on his car.* It wouldn't be enough, but it would be satisfying to watch him cleaning literal shit. I daydream about killing him…the life draining from his eyes as they stare into my own. Now *that* would be satisfying.

I allow the daydream to curl the ends of my lips into a rare smile. It is only a dream. I will not do it. Not because of some moral compass that would not allow me to do it. No, I can convince myself that he deserves it quite easily.

I will not do it. Simply, because of Marnie. All of this is because of Marnie. Every moment of my life has been because of her. I will not spend my life locked in a prison cell, away from her. That would be throwing away everything of meaning in my life.

But a man can dream.

Chapter Forty-Seven

One Month Ago

Sleep is becoming near impossible. I am convinced I have given myself stomach ulcers from all the worry and a black coffee only diet. My guts are in constant pain and I imagine my intestines twisting around themselves over and over until the whole thing is nothing more than one big knot.

The benefit of not taking care of myself, is that I have lost some weight. While I would not have called myself out of shape before, I admit now that I had a small beer belly. A bit of a dad bod, minus the kids. Yet another thing Billy had bested me on. A lack of food and excess of stress has been my friend in this case, my stomach now looking equal to the man who has everything…including my wife.

I sit at the yellowing Formica kitchen table we use as a dining table, mail drop zone and occasional kitchen counter. No long walnut dining table in a massive perfect house for us. It irks me that Billy will always have that over my head, no matter how much I try to mimic myself to him physically.

The coffee now wrapped in my hands has gone cold. No matter. It is more of a prop at this point. Something to occupy my hands while I wait for Marnie to leave for work, wait to leave behind her so I can watch what this day has in store for her.

"What the hell is this?" Marnie enters the kitchen, waving an envelope in her hand.

Even from here, I can see the familiar red lettering stamped across the white of the envelope. *Past Due.*

"What's wrong, babe?" She catches me off guard and I am unable to make up a lie so quickly. I will have to play dumb.

"Why is the electric bill past due?" She asks. Her hand waves the envelope angrily, those beautiful green eyes narrowed and glaring.

"I must have forgotten to pay it, sorry babe. I'll get it figured out today." I stand as I speak, walking to the sink to wash out my coffee mug.

"And the mortgage? Did you forget to pay that too?" Her hand is on her hip, her voice becoming more accusing.

I take my time washing the chipped mug, unable to look into those eyes any longer. I hate to lie…and I hate that she doesn't seem to mind it.

"I must have. Sorry." I say quietly, wanting this interaction to end before she digs any further.

"For two months?" She replies.

I realize then that this is not a spur of the moment argument, this is a planned ambush. She knows that something is not right with me. Is she ready to admit what is not right with *her*? I guess my silence stretches longer than she finds acceptable because she no longer awaits my response.

"Did you lose your job?" She has always been blunt. Someone to get right to the point. It is one of the things I have always loved about her. Today, I curse it. She is forcing me to lie or come clean.

"Yes." I whisper. I stare down into the kitchen sink at my lone mug, now cleaner than it has been in months.

"Why didn't you tell me? You have been acting funny for a while now. You have been distant emotionally, acting jumpy and jittery, spending nearly all your time out of the house, then the nose job. Now I find out you aren't even working. Where have you been all these nights that you say you are working overtime? You have not been yourself lately Max…what is going on?"

So much to unpack there. So much I want to shout, want to throw in her face and turn it all on her. Isn't it always the way, people seeing the way you change without accepting it is their behavior that has inspired your change? A sudden pressure in my head and my brain is pounding against my skull. For a minute, I think my brain is about to explode. I cannot hold it in any longer.

It is killing me.

Marnie is killing me.

"You see the changes in me. Do you see the changes in yourself, Marnie?" My voice is only slightly above a whisper. I force a calm that I do not feel.

"Don't turn this on me. We are talking about you. We are talking about you losing your job and saying nothing to me. *Your wife.*" She hisses.

"My wife." I repeat the words with disgust before a laugh escapes my lips. "My wife, who has been *fucking* someone else for nearly a year. My wife who has the *nerve* to scold me about secrets."

Marnie's jaw drops open, the shock clear on her face. She really believed I didn't know. She really had no idea that I have been following them the entire time. Her lips begin to move, looking for the right words. Even the best words would be poison to me right now. I do not want her attempts to justify anything. I want to be heard.

I speak again before she can. "You see the changes in me, and you ask why. I have known about your affair for eleven months. Eleven months of waiting for regret, or some small speck of respect for me to kick in. I have searched my brain for every way that I can be better, for you. You ask why I got a nose job…it is for you. He has a perfect nose. That's what you want, isn't it? He doesn't have a beer belly. Now I don't either. I can dye my hair, tan my skin. I have tried to change myself physically to please you…to be what you so clearly want. I don't know why he is better than me mentally, but I can change that too. I can *be* whatever it is you want, Marnie. I will *do* whatever you want, Marnie. You are my everything, and even now, I don't have a single strand of hate for you. I just want everything to go back to what we were. Just us."

"He is not better than you." She whispers, tearing streaming down her cheeks.

"Then end it. I will never speak of it again. End it and fix us, and I will forgive everything."

It is a simple request, and a huge undertaking. It will linger in my mind for a long time, I know that. But I will swallow my pride for as long as I need to if it means everything can be wonderful again. Just the two of us, in our tiny, cozy home, laughing at our Formica kitchen table. I see it now. We don't have much, yet we have everything. Something Billy will never have. True, unbreakable love. I am richer than he could ever hope to be. I feel the pieces of my heart slowly mending back together at the realization.

"Deal."

"Really?"

"Yes, I will end it with him today. I promise."

Chapter Forty-Eight

Three Weeks Ago

The biggest regret I will ever experience in my life, is that I did not follow Marnie that day, one week ago. I believed her. *I know her.* If she wasn't going to end it with Billy, she would not have said that she would.

The excitement of our pending repair had begun to heal me the moment her promise was made. I spent the day cleaning the house and preparing dinner for Marnie's return. An hour after she would normally be home from work, the dinner already cold, I began to worry. Had her promise been a lie? Had she chosen *him*? Maybe in her attempt to end it, he promised her things I could never give her. Financial security being the main guess. Money is a powerful persuasion tool.

I feel so much guilt for letting those thoughts enter my head in those early moments. Did I lose precious time that changed everything?

It has been one week since that conversation with Marnie. After leaving our home, she went to her brother Nikolas' house and dropped off his weekly Tupperware meals. There is no evidence of it, but I know she then met with Billy to break it off. She never arrived at work that day.

The police do not believe me. They don't believe Marnie was having an affair, since there is no evidence of it. Even her phone records are clean of anything relating to Billy. I have no idea how they contacted each other; there must have been a second phone. I give police as much information about him as I can, without ever admitting to my stalking. They do not believe me. Police believe I am attempting to create a diversion, creating some imaginary man to take the fall for my wife's disappearance.

According to them, it must have been Nikolas or me. *Always the husband.* Everyone knows that. Nikolas is simply thrown in because he was the last known person to see her. Sure, that makes it likely, but the police already have their man. Me. Always the husband.

Except this time.

This time, it was *not* the husband.

It was the lover.

I just have to prove it.

Chapter Forty-Nine

Three Weeks Ago

Luckily, I have had a year of experience following Billy. I already know the ins and outs of this man's life, and at this point I have nothing to lose. I know that he has killed my wife. If only I had followed her that day, everything would be different.

The prickly bush is at it again, attacking my exposed skin, as I stare into the dining room of Billy's perfect life. His perfect wife waits on him as if she is his personal maid, and his lips only part to shovel undoubtedly delicious food into his stupid mouth. A rage emerges deep within me. I want this man dead. But

I cannot kill him. Not so long as he is the only person to know where my wife is.

I have been following Billy's every waking moment since the realization that Marnie is truly missing. His schedule has remained pretty routine. He has not missed a day of work, a dinner with his wife, or a visit to the second home he used to play house with my wife. Has he already gotten rid of Marnie? *I should have followed her that day.* I get the feeling that will be the biggest regret of my life. I will never forgive myself.

While I continue to watch the ice cold couple eat their dinner silently, I accept that Marnie cannot be anywhere near this house. I don't know if she was even aware that Billy was married, or had another home.

No, she is not here.

He would not blow up this portion of his life.

This is the life he shows the world.

Marnie is the life he keeps hidden.

Just like the home surrounded by so much overgrowth, it is a secret, even from the neighbors. This man would kill to keep my wife his dirty little secret. I have no doubt about that. I may be too late to save

Marnie's life, but I will not rest until her body is home with her family, where she belongs.

Chapter Fifty

Two Weeks Ago

I have no idea if this is going to work.

I have to try. The nose job has done me wonders, but there are still small differences between us. I stand in aisle seven at the drugstore, staring at an entire wall of hair dye choices. Why are there so many choices? I have never done this before and I find my heart aching for Marnie. She would have found me the perfect color ten minutes ago.

Instead, I stand here until every shade of brown looks the exact same, then choose one that I am sure is darker than my own. My lungs crave a sigh of relief, but no relief comes as I move down the aisle and stare at the at home perm kits. This is going to be much harder on me to do myself, but Billy's hair is a clump of messy waves that don't seem at all styled, so I am hopeful that my lack of skills will still produce a similar result.

Two boxes of baffling hair products in hand, I check out and head to the tanning salon in the same plaza. Luckily, I have olive skin naturally, so it should only take a session or two before I return to my natural sun kissed glow.

I complete my transformation before Billy leaves his office for the day and follow him home to his perfect life.

I know he does not see me, but I find myself being extra careful this time. Before the makeover, I was just some similar looking guy who happened to be in the same vicinity as him. Now, I could be his twin. The tan and hair changes, along with the colored contact lenses I ordered a few weeks ago, did more for me than I even expected, and I felt sick as I stared into the bathroom mirror. I wanted to smash that mirror underneath my fist.

The red-haired woman, who is undoubtedly his wife, once again serves him dinner as if he is the king himself. From my vantage point of the dining room window, I cannot smell anything, but I am willing to bet that lasagna smells as delicious as it looks. She must be a hell of a cook.

After setting down the dish of still bubbling lasagna, she returns to the kitchen. I am unable to see much, but based on the countertops I can see, I imagine it is a magazine worthy kitchen. She returns, carrying a glass, which she sets down in front of Billy. He doesn't even say thank you. He barely even glances in her direction. How does a man like that get his wife, *and* mine?

He sips his drink slowly, but deeply. As he sets the glass down, I notice more than half of the dark liquid is gone already. He seems so calm, in no rush at all. There isn't a single trace of guilt on his face, as if my wife's life meant exactly nothing. I know he must have hidden her in the second house that appears to be secret from even his wife. I have to get the keys to that house.

Now that I look just like Billy, I should be able to find an opportune moment to get his keys without a second thought from anyone around. I should be able to get into that house without a second thought from any possible prying eyes. Sure, I could just break in…but I don't want to alert Billy to my suspicions. If Marnie isn't in that house, I still need to follow Billy long enough to find her.

I will not let her rot away in some unmarked grave courtesy of this man. She deserves better than that…even if her actions have shattered me.

Suddenly, Billy falls from his chair, hitting the floor with a loud thud. I sit up from my hiding spot, getting a better view of the man now lying on the floor. His body begins to shake violently and our eyes lock. He is looking right at me. Does he see me? My brain is telling me to duck into the shadows once again but my body does not move. He is having a seizure, and I cannot look away. His body stills.

Billy clutches his chest, mouth gaping, gasping desperately for air. His wife stands in the doorway to the kitchen, staring down at her husband who is clearly in need of immediate medical attention. Her face is completely blank.

As he clutches his chest, his body shakes again, and I am consumed by the thought that he is staring into my soul. Does he see me at all or are his eyes simply staring forward, into nothingness? I glance between his obvious medical emergency and his unimpressed wife until Billy stills completely.

The wife then leans down, her two fingers touching his neck. I can hear my heartbeat pounding loudly in my ears and I feel like she might hear it too. How could she not? It is the loudest sound I have ever heard. Her fingers move to his wrist. Still, she exhibits no emotion on her face. Her fingers then move to the underside of Billy's nostrils. She is checking if he is breathing.

There is no panic. There is no rush to call for an ambulance. There is no sadness, or desperation.

She rises from her bent position and moves toward the dining table. She clutches Billy's glass in her hand tightly and returns to the kitchen, stepping over Billy's crumpled body.

I stare into Billy's open eyes, now surely unseeing. My body is frozen and my mind is running a mile a minute.

He is dead.

Billy is dead.

The woman returns, dragging something large behind her. She bends to pick it up and lift it into the dining room. She then sets down a long sled next to Billy's body and bends again, rolling him onto the waiting ride. I am struck by the stillness of her face. There is no panic at all. No regret. Simply, a methodical act, as if she has done this a million times before. Billy must have been even worse to her than I assumed.

She disappears from view, Billy's body in tow behind her. I scurry from my familiar hiding spot, staying close to the house as I rush toward the side door. I crouch down near another shrub and watch as the side door opens and the beautiful woman pulling Billy's lifeless body emerges from the home.

I don't dare move as I watch the woman dragging the sled, walking slowly toward the woods behind their house. My eyes refuse to leave Billy's body, as if I expect him to jump up suddenly, all of this being nothing more than some terrible prank or misunderstanding. I watch until his feet disappear from my sight, into the woods.

A deep sigh escapes me and I suddenly feel very alone. The woman killed Billy. He is dead. I should be celebrating. Instead, a fear grows inside me, the fear that he has the answer I need so desperately, that I will now never hear.

I snap myself out of the fog quickly and realize this is my only chance. Billy is gone. I can now get his keys and check the other house for Marnie. His keys are probably inside this house right now. I stare at the wood line, searching for any movement indicating that Billy's wife is returning. There is a complete stillness that somehow feels even more unsettling. I shudder at the realization of everything I have just witnessed. I wanted Billy dead in so many moments, but there was something very unsettling about witnessing the whole thing in this way.

I shake my head forcefully, hoping all these thoughts escape my brain, simply fall from my ears and never return. This man killed my wife. He deserved everything he got. Hell, he deserved remaining conscious while I beat in his skull until his brains were scattered around the room. His end was more merciful than he deserved.

The mudroom door closes noiselessly behind me and I tiptoe through the kitchen that I had only seen bits and pieces of from the dining room window. My knowledge of the layout of this house is limited, but I assume the bedrooms are upstairs so I locate the staircase quickly and begin my ascend.

Once I locate the master bedroom, I quickly search the nightstand drawers. I squeeze my hand tightly around Billy's keys, fully expecting them to try to escape my grip. It feels too easy.

A quick scan out the window proves that the wife is still busy disposing of Billy's corpse and I am alone. I might as well make the most of this opportunity, so I begin searching Billy's belongings. There is a chance I will find something that helps me in my search for Marnie.

As I enter his walk-in closet, I begin looking through the clothes hanging in front of me. A familiar smell fills my nostrils and I realize it is the smell that has lived on Marnie this past year. *His* smell. Hot burning rage fills me. It creeps up my neck as I daydream about the death that Billy deserved. I always knew it would end in his death…I just assumed the blood would be on my hands.

The rage immediately turns to ice as a new realization occurs to me. What if Marnie is not in the other house? I finally have the keys, but this could be a dead end. I have no other ideas of where she could be. I planned to follow him until I found her, but that is no longer an option. How can I get closer to him now that he is dead?

I can become him.

Why not? There is nothing left of my own life now. The only thing that matters anymore is finding my wife. What other way is there at this point? If I become Billy, I can literally walk in his shoes. I can go everywhere I have watched him go, I can talk to anyone he knows, I can learn parts of him that stalking never gave me.

It is the only option, and I am ready.

I look just like him. I know his schedule. I know the basics of his life. I don't want his life. I want my wife. I will live his life until I find her body. I just need a few days, a week or so, tops.

His wife has given me this gift. Sure, she will know that I am not Billy. But who can she tell? She just murdered her husband. It's not like she can tell the police how she knows that I am not Billy. She would have to prove it.

It is in this moment that I decide to become an imposter.

Chapter Fifty-One

Two Weeks Ago

There is a terrifying thrill coursing through my body as I listen to Billy's wife in the bedroom. I sit on the floor of the walk-in closet, shoved into a deep corner, underneath a pile of unfolded clothes. The smell of Billy is the only thing that fills my nostrils and I feel as murderous as his wife must feel right now. Am I absolutely crazy? Have I done the right thing?

I breathe easier as I hear the running water of the shower, his wife surely washing off the dirt of whatever makeshift grave she dug. I find myself holding my breath when I hear her footsteps near the closet door and pray that she has no need to look in here. I tried my best to cover myself from view, but I imagine the lumpy pile of clothes looks far from normal.

My prayers are answered as the footsteps continue to another area of the bedroom. I imagine she will be asleep very soon, so I wait patiently until I hear nothing but her deep breathing and the occasional soft snore.

The closet door inches open very slowly. I can't chance any creaking and there is no rush. I take my time with the endeavor, only breathing normally once I am beside her in bed, her breathing still deep and unbothered.

I imagine lying here all night, only pretending to sleep if she stirs, but find my eyelids growing too heavy to fight. Within moments, the snores of us both fill the room.

Chapter Fifty-Two

Seven Days Ago

I almost feel bad for taking Billy's place. Not because he is dead, that I am still happy about. No, it is because of his wife, Katherine. She really is lovely, and I hope that she isn't losing it mentally over my sudden appearance after Billy's murder. She is stronger than she realizes, and I know she will be okay. I do my best to be aware of her feelings in all of this. I don't want to hurt her, but this is the only way to find Marnie.

It is important that I continue following Billy's schedule uninterrupted. The last thing we need is for anyone to realize that I am not Billy, or worse, that the real Billy is missing. Katherine did what she had to do, and frankly, he deserved much worse. She did him a favor, really. I would not have shown so much mercy.

The first thing I did was check the second house. I searched everywhere within the house, even under furniture and in the attic. There is no trace of Marnie. I nearly walked away from this whole thing, until Nikolas convinced me that I have to take advantage of this opportunity. I can't accept that I may not find my wife. I can't give up on her.

Nikolas is right though. I have been presented with a unique situation. A few days of planning between us and I have created a backup plan. Any trace of possible evidence of Marnie's killing, or their affair, needs to be staged in the second house. If evidence does not exist, I will plant it. I already look like Billy, so I will go to the local hardware store and purchase all the things I imagine one would need to dispose of a dead body. Not only will those things be staged in the second house, but Billy is now seen in town buying some very suspicious items.

Once I am finished doing everything I can to make Billy look guilty, the police will be forced to accept that Billy is responsible for Marnie's disappearance, even if they will never find him. I wouldn't do that to Katherine. She doesn't deserve punishment for ridding the world of that stain…she deserves a medal.

Instead, I will let the police believe that he is on the run. Hopefully, they will have more luck finding my sweet Marnie's body than I have.

At the very least, I will clear myself and Nikolas from police suspicion. I may have no life left without her, but Nikolas deserves to piece together whatever life he can after all of this.

Chapter Fifty-Three

One Day Ago

The house is staged. The murder kit has been placed around the property and a clump of Marnie's hair, courtesy of her hair brush, has been scattered around both the house and car. Her DNA will be here when the police come, whether her body is or not. I don't care if Billy managed to leave behind zero evidence of her murder, I will make sure the police have enough to know he must be responsible. If I am lucky, maybe they will dig up the entire property searching for her.

Beyond the physical evidence at the home, I made sure to leave a suspicious little trail around town.

The hardware store receipt, now located in the nightstand drawer, will show where I purchased all the items now located in this house. I also made sure to have some memorable conversation with the cashier, asking if they carried any products meant to dissolve bone. He was clearly taken back, so I quickly mentioned it was for animals, of course. I then made sure to tell a long story about a deer carcass that has begun to attract bears. He will remember me when the police come asking, I am sure of that.

After finding a receipt from some swanky restaurant in the pocket of one of Billy's jackets, I went to the location to continue being as suspicious as possible. I slipped a waitress some money to pretend I had never been there, ensuring I mentioned that I don't want my wife to find out about my lover. As any woman would, she seemed pretty taken back by the request to hide my affair, but a hundred-dollar bill convinced her to agree. That girl will sing like a canary when the police come sniffing around. As she should, honestly. I did my best to come off like a real creep. What can I say? Billy inspired me.

Just to add some icing on the cake, I made sure to casually mention to the pig Billy calls his coworker that I had been having an affair. He didn't seem surprised, but it was obviously news to him. Clearly, Marnie was meant to always be a secret. It hurt my heart to speak about her so casually, like she wasn't God's greatest creation. I couldn't go as far as that pig wanted, requesting details that should only remain between two people. It was the worst lunch of my life. I left swearing that I would never find myself alone with that sorry excuse for a man again.

I am finding it hard to accept that this charade will have to end soon. Katherine is lovely, and I find myself hoping that we will remain friends once this is all over. I don't feel ready to be alone. I don't feel ready to face my inevitable grief.

I know it is an impossible dream, because I do not think she had any idea about Billy's affair. I can only imagine what she is going through right now, with the act of murder and an imposter's presence in her life. The last thing I want is to make it harder. Everything left will crumble when the police inform her of what Billy did...but she will be free.

Free of Billy, and free of the charge of murder hanging over her head.

I am doing this for her, as much as myself.

PART THREE

Present Day

Chapter Fifty-Four

Present Day

Katherine

My body remains rigid, seemingly frozen in this moment, while my mind races faster than I can process. I believe everything Max has said, yet the confirmation of the kind of man Billy was is extremely unsettling. For so many years, I assumed *I* was the problem.

The girl who just couldn't seem to fit into the mold laid out for her. The same mold that so many women in my life have happily settled in to.

I assumed that was reason enough for Billy and I to be unhappy. I just wasn't what I should have been, wasn't what he expected when he married me. I stand here realizing I had been comparing myself to nothing more than a livestock purchase. He bought the cow, but the dang thing just refused to stay in its pen.

It was never me.

I simply wanted a life that made me happy. Billy wanted property. He wanted a maid, a chef, a servant, someone who would plaster on a fake smile and show the world that he had it all…and some.

I played right into it, simply because I didn't know any better. All these years and it took this very moment to lift this weight off of me, to finally jump start waking up.

Max is standing so still, he is momentarily forgotten. Here I am, realizing the implications of everything Billy has done had on my life, but what about Max?

Max lost a wife. Not in the way that I lost a husband, one who had weighed me down, a loss that can be celebrated.

No, Max has experienced a loss that is devastating. Billy took from him something that no one can ever give back.

“I’m so sorry for what Billy has done.” I whisper, unsure of what else to say after so much has been spilled between us.

Max releases a deep sigh, and I am not sure if it is from relief or pain. Maybe both. “You have nothing to say sorry for. You are just as much a victim as Marnie is.”

“I am a murderer.” I state boldly. I have never tried the words out loud before, and it feels good to finally admit it to someone, even someone who already knew it.

“You are a woman who improved the world, in a horrific act that was forced upon you.”

“I don’t want you to justify it. I could have divorced him. I should have divorced him. Now I will give up the rest of my life because of him. In the end, he got what he wanted…my whole life in the palm of his hand.” I stare at my own feet. I am ashamed that I once again have played right into Billy’s hand.

Even when he is dead, he still controls my life.

“They will never find his body.”

My head whips upward so fast, I feel the vertebrae in my neck crack. "It *was* you. You moved his body."

"The less you know, the better."

I can't help but smile. There is nothing happy about our situations right now, but in this moment, I realize that Max is truly my friend. He has taken care of me in ways far deeper than Billy ever did. He has helped me to see all the things I had become blind to.

"Thank you." I squeak. It doesn't feel like enough, but it is all I can say. Kindness still feels foreign.

"He may have ruined my life, and taken Marnie's, but that's where it ends. He no longer controls yours. Now, I have to finish staging this house before I make an anonymous tip to the police about Billy. If everything plays out the way I have planned, Billy will become prime suspect and I will be free of suspicion. Police will think he made a run for it, and you will be free of any suspicion in his disappearance. We will both be able to rebuild our lives the best we can, though I admit, I think you have a much better shot at it than I do."

"What about finding Marnie?" I ask quietly, I am unable to add the word *body*.

"I have looked through the entire house. I have checked the property for any upturned dirt. I have to accept she isn't here. Maybe the police will have better luck bringing her body home to me."

I think back to when Billy and I stood in this very spot, the night of one of Uncle Ted's parties. Billy was right that I had been drinking, and laughing quite a bit, but I was enthralled with the way that Uncle Ted saw the world. He was somewhat of a doomsday believer and loved to ramble down the hole of various conspiracy theories. It always angered Billy, but I loved hearing the mysteries and theories of the world. It was one of the few times I saw how vast things were outside of my tiny bubble.

If you could believe it, I have my very own bunker. Yup, I'm ready for when the world comes to its inevitable end, Kitty Kat. You can join me down there too; I always liked ya. Good conversation, this one.

The bunker.

I rush toward the kitchen, shoving Max out of the doorway in my haste.

"Damn, Katherine, what the hell?" I hear him sulk from behind me.

"Help me!" I shout, unable to make my brain take the time to explain anything.

I hear his footsteps behind me as I grab hold of the kitchen island and begin to push. It is so heavy, it barely moves an inch. Uncle Ted was definitely much stronger than I am.

"What are you doing?" Max asks.

"Help me move this thing!" I shout.

He bends beside me, grabbing the corner of the countertop and bracing his feet. He begins to push and the large island moves gracefully across the kitchen floor.

I turn back to the hatch now revealed in the middle of the floor.

"Uncle Ted had a bomb shelter."

Chapter Fifty-Five

Max pushes his way in front of me and yanks the large metal hatch with all his might. The door swings up and nearly smacks him right in the face. The near miss doesn't seem to faze him at all as he begins to descend the dark staircase.

I scurry behind him, grabbing the back of his shirt so we don't lose each other in the overwhelming darkness. While our descent is incredibly slow, feeling cautiously for each next step, heading into the unknown, it seems this staircase is much longer than any other I have ever climbed. How deep is this thing?

I know my mind is playing tricks on me, but I can't help but feel a pang of fear. I am glad Max admitted to moving Billy's body, otherwise my overactive imagination might conjure up his zombie form down here in the darkness.

I can hear the sharp, quick breaths coming out of Max and I know he too is feeling scared. I wonder if it is the fear of the darkness and the unknown…or the fear of possibly being in the same room as his wife's dead body.

Our footsteps clunk onto the concrete floor, we have reached the bottom of the staircase. I begin feeling on the wall, looking for a light switch. Uncle Ted was so into preparedness; I have to assume this bunker is equipped with electricity. The sound of Max's footsteps continues into the room, and I have to remind my brain that it is him to avoid panicking alone in the dark.

After what feels like an eternity, I locate a small protrusion from the wall and acknowledge the familiar feel of a light switch. I flip the switch and sigh as relief floods through my anxiety ridden bones. The room fills with warm, buzzing light.

I turn to find Max standing in the center of the room, his back to me, eyes fixed to the wall directly in front of him. He falls to his knees, shuddering sobs escaping, eyes never leaving that wall.

My fixation with Max is only broken by the sound of metal clacking. I too look to the wall before Max, to the large metal chains dangling and swaying. My eyes follow those chains to the small body seated against the wall, her sunken eyes staring straight into the Imposter's.

"Max, is that you?" Her voice daring to journey out of her scratchy throat and parched lips.

"My Marnie!" The voice that erupts from Max is unlike any I have ever heard, and I realize that he too must have thought Marnie was dead, her corpse still chained to the wall. Her sunken face and matted hair are very corpse-like. I immediately feel guilty for that thought, especially considering *my* husband put her here.

He leaps toward her, wrapping her in his arms as they both release gasping sobs, uttering words that I cannot, and try not to hear. It is a moment that I feel wholly outside of, and a strong desire to leave the room nearly overcomes me. As I near the staircase, Max suddenly turns to me, tears streaming down his joyous face.

"You gave me my wife back. I owe you everything." He whispers.

I wave my hand, motioning that it was no big deal, feeling uncapable of words in this moment.

Max turns back to Marnie, wrapping his fingers around the thick chain holding his wife hostage. He follows the chains, both leading to a single padlock.

"Did Uncle Ted have any bolt cutters?" He asks, clearly having gone into fix it mode.

"I have no idea." I say meekly.

Max takes off running for the stairs, likely going to the shed in the backyard to investigate our options.

I approach Marnie, suddenly realizing that I have been watching her like some chained circus animal.

I am somehow responsible for this.

I should have known Billy was cheating, I should have put an end to it.

I should have known Billy was capable of this. I should have put an end to it so much sooner.

"I'm sorry Billy did this to you." I whisper, stepping toward her slowly, as if she may bite at any moment.

"Did the police get him?" She asks. Her voice sounds so painful, I consider going to get her water before even answering. I decide she probably needs that answer, even more than water right now.

"He's dead." I say flatly. Even now I can't manage to put any emotion into those words.

"Good." A response so simple. No need for how or why, instead simple satisfaction with the ultimate end.

I can tell I am going to like Marnie.

Chapter Fifty-Six

Before Max returns from the shed, I remember the three other unknown keys in my pocket. It can't hurt to try while we wait. The third key slides in effortlessly just as Max returns to the bunker.

"Do you have the key?" He is out of breath.

"It looks like it." My reply coming out more sarcastic than I intended.

The lock opens with a loud click and Marnie immediately pulls at the chains, causing them to fall from their brackets. I then try the remaining two keys on the lockbox connecting her handcuffs to the chains, near her stomach. I successfully open the black box, then use the remaining strangely shaped key to open her handcuffs.

She is free.

Max and Marnie embrace long enough that I feel that extreme awkwardness again. This time, I do leave the room.

When they finally return upstairs, I have a large glass of water waiting for Marnie. She gulps it down in two seconds flat. I fill it again; this time she paces herself.

In the time they were downstairs reuniting, I have come up with a plan. As I explain it to the two of them, they both nod along eagerly.

Billy may be dead, but I just don't think that was enough.

Chapter Fifty-Seven

Max and Marnie say their goodbyes and he leaves Uncle Ted's house, planning to return Billy's car to my house, then go home to his own. He will need to get to work altering his appearance again.

Marnie and I wait in the kitchen, the island still pulled into the corner, the hatch door open. After we have given enough time for Max to get home, we ready ourselves for an Oscar winning performance. It only takes ten minutes before the entire property is swarming with police officers. Officers begin searching the bunker, each of the rooms inside the home, and the property outside. I watch as the evidence Max planted is bagged and labeled.

Marnie and I are separated to tell our portions of the story, which we had expected. I sit on the back patio with a man named Detective Jenkins and explain how I found Marnie.

"I woke up this morning and Billy was gone. We didn't have a fight, or anything like that. I was actually really worried that something had happened to him. His phone and car were still at home, so I thought maybe he was with friends. When he didn't come home by dinner, I decided to go out looking for him. I wasn't really sure where to look, since he doesn't go out much, and the hunting lodge is closed at that time of night. I figured maybe he stayed here, at Uncle Ted's house. Maybe he was mad at me for somethin' I didn't realize, or maybe he just needed some space. He isn't a sharer; I sometimes have no idea how he is feeling." I feel my southern accent thickening and I take full advantage of it. Men love a woman with a southern accent, especially here in the south. It reminds them of their Mamas, and most didn't have Mamas like mine.

Lucky them.

"What happened when you arrived here?" Detective Jenkins asks, his pen poised above the notebook balanced on his knee.

"Well, I had to try a couple of keys that were unfamiliar to me because I hadn't been here since right after Uncle Ted passed. Billy took care of this place. Once I was inside, I walked around, figuring I would find Billy sleeping on the couch, or in one of the bedrooms. I thought maybe he had a little binge the night before, he sometimes did that to blow off some steam, you know."

"But he wasn't here?" The detective asks, prompting me to continue.

"No, he wasn't. So, of course, I start to get worried sick. As I walked around the bedroom, I started seeing some stuff that had me real scared."

"What kind of stuff, ma'am?"

"Oh, just call me Katherine, Officer. Well. I saw wrapping for one of those big blue tarps all laid out on the ground and duct tape near it. There was a gas can just sitting near the back door. Why would there be a gas can in the house, you know? I started to get really scared, like maybe Billy was being held here against his will. Maybe he was kidnapped."

"So, then what did you do?"

"Well, I made sure to look *everywhere* in the house, but there was no Billy. So of course, I'm panicking and about to call y'all to come take a missing person report when I remembered that Uncle Ted was one of those doomsday types. Always a bit weird for our taste, but he's family, so we loved him all the same."

"Of course."

"So, then I thought maybe I should check the bunker, just to be thorough before I call y'all out here. I wouldn't want to waste police time."

"We appreciate that, ma'am. Describe what you saw when you went in the bunker."

"Well, it took some time for me to get that far, you know. That kitchen island is heavy. Luckily, I was so worried Billy was somehow trapped in there, it wasn't too hard to muster up all my strength. After I got in there, I had to feel around for the light switch for a minute before I finally found the dang thing. Once the light was on, I saw that woman…chained up to the wall."

I begin to softly cry. The detective pats my shoulder a few times and hands me a tissue.

"Take your time, ma'am."

"It was just awful. Just awful. She was chained up like an animal…and so thin! Like the poor thing hadn't had anything to eat! It took me some time but I managed to figure out which key from Billy's keyring opened the padlocks. She said Billy abducted her. Said he was going to *kill* her." I whisper the last part, more for effect than anything.

The detective's pen moves furiously over his notepad. I can hear the gentle scratching against the paper as I continue talking.

"How could Billy do this, Officer? Why is this happening? Where is he?"

My questions seem to echo in the silence, the scratching noise of the pen still dancing between us.

"Thank you so much, Katherine. I hope you know that you saved Marnie's life today."

"Oh, I don't want any credit for that. I just praise God that he put me in the right place at the right time."

Chapter Fifty-Eight

Marnie

"Start from the beginning. What happened the day of your abduction?" The detective asks, his dark eyes boring into my soul.

"Well, the beginning would have been a year before that…when I started seeing Billy."

"Seeing him? You mean, dating?"

"More like casual sex. At least, for me, that's all it was."

"Okay, so you were having casual sex with him for a year before your abduction."

"Yeah, just about. But then my husband, Max, confronted me about the affair."

"Was he angry?"

"No. He was hurt. He said if I broke it off, then he would forgive everything and we could work on our marriage."

"That's what you wanted?" He looks skeptical, like being found chained up in the man's doomsday bunker isn't enough to take the suspicion off of my husband. *It's always the husband*…apparently even when the lover leaves you to die in his bunker.

"More than anything, honestly. The affair started right after my mother died. I wasn't myself. It was a terrible mistake that just spiraled. I never had feelings for Billy; it was just a release from my actual life." I stare down into my hands. I feel so much guilt for what I have done to Max. Even more for Katherine, who was the key to saving me today.

"Did you break up with Billy?"

"Right after Max confronted me. I had to go to work, but I left the house early. I stopped at my brother Nikolas' house to drop off some food. He hasn't been taking care of himself since our mother died, and I feel responsible for making sure he is okay. After that, I met Billy here, on my way to work. I told him I was done, that we couldn't meet up anymore. He hit me so hard, I must have went unconscious. I woke up already chained in the bunker. I was so groggy, I know it wasn't just the hit…he must have drugged me or something."

"We can test for anything in your system."

"Okay. That's good."

"What happened while you were chained in the bunker?"

"He was so angry. It was like a completely different person, like something in him just snapped. He wasn't in control anymore and he had to change that. He fed me and visited me the first few days. He taunted me. It felt like he was keeping me alive just to prove he could, prove it was his choice what happened between us. Then about a day or two ago, he told me he was going to kill me that night." I can't stop the tears burning hot streaks down my cheeks. I know I will have to relive these moments a hundred more times before it is over, and I pray that it gets easier.

"What happened when he came back that night?" The detective's voice is low; he sits perched on the edge of his chair.

"He never did. I thought maybe he had changed his mind. Maybe he was going to let me starve to death instead. Maybe it was all just another game to show me that he was the one in control."

The detective leans forward over his notebook, scribbling whatever notes he found important enough to quote.

I lean forward, whispering my next question. "Are you going to get him? He will kill me if he finds me."

"One of our detectives is with a magistrate now. We are getting a warrant for his arrest. We will find him. He can't hurt you anymore, Marnie."

At this, I begin to sob, and silently thank Katherine for giving me that gift.

Billy is dead.

Chapter Fifty-Nine

Katherine

I allowed police complete access to Uncle Ted's home and all of Billy's belongings in my own house, not that they didn't easily get a search warrant. In fact, I told them to take everything of his they possibly could. I couldn't stomach to ever see it again. It is easy to appear like the scorned wife; my anger is no façade. It's like everything I have held in for years finally has an outlet. Finally, the mask is removed and the whole world sees Billy for who he really was.

My house did not yield many results for the police, thankfully. The last thing I need is to live in a crime scene. Uncle Ted's house on the other hand, was a treasure trove of evidence…and not just the stuff Max and I planted. The evidence relating to Marnie would have been quite scarce without our help, but the police would not have had a shortage of items to prove what a creep Billy actually was. It turns out that he had been hiding an entire collection of trophies that police are now linking to various missing persons cases.

So far, he has been linked to the disappearance of three women from neighboring areas. Police believe he may have been a serial killer, though they are yet to find any actual bodies. It sure is odd though for him to have a collection of their jewelry and underwear, if he isn't actually responsible for them being missing.

While Max insists that this is even more reason to feel no guilt for his murder, I cannot help but feel even more consumed with what I have done. Billy was likely the only person who knew where these women are, and I feel drowning guilt for their families. If I had known, perhaps I could have tortured it out of him before I killed him. Max reminds me that I am not like him. I would not have tortured another human being. I remind him that I have killed one…I might be more like him than I want to admit.

The police still believe that Billy is on the run, and I am stuck in a very strange place. The properties are in both our names, so I am unable to sell. I would rather no one believe Billy is dead, so I can't try to have him legally declared dead, at least for a very long time.

So, I am still living in the home we shared together, the home that became the scene of his murder. I don't mind though, as it really is a beautiful house. I plan to redecorate entirely once I have some more disposable income. Until then, I have done my best to scrub the Billy out of it.

I haven't quite figured out my life yet, and I realize that is okay. Most people my age have had an entire decade of building behind them, and I am just starting out. It is okay to go at my pace and figure out what is right for me.

In the meantime, I got a job at a bakery, and it pays well enough to cover all the bills and buy me plenty of lipstick. The best part is, I get to decide where my money goes.

I get to decide everything in my life now.

Max and Marnie returned to their life as if none of this ever happened. The moment he returned home after finding Marnie, he shaved his head and took out his colored contacts. A few days of facial hair growth, and he barely resembled Billy anymore. Well, he could have been mistaken for a cousin, not for the man himself.

They both play a big part in my life now, and for the first time, I have true friends I can rely on. The two of them come for dinner often, and I promise to never serve diet coke. Or, if I do, I at least have the decency to bring them the unopened can.

Their love is almost sickening, like watching two school kids discovering the opposite sex for the first time. In some ways, it is inspiring though. I hope I can find what they have some day. Just not any time soon. I've had enough husband for quite a while.

The title of murderer will never be washed from me, but I am learning to accept it. When I look at everything that has happened, everything that my life is becoming, I admit that I would not want it any other way.

Billy is dead, and I no longer have to be an imposter in my own life.

I have *the* imposter to thank for that.

Chapter Sixty

Max

The past year has been pretty rough on everyone.

Okay, *really* rough on everyone. It still feels unbelievable that Marnie is alive. I had accepted that Billy killed her, but never gave up on finding her body. If I had not insisted on that, she would have died in that bunker of dehydration. I shudder at the thought of my wife suffering like that.

Marnie's family had been broken by the loss of her mother, but were irrevocably shattered by our belief that Marnie was dead. I couldn't help but feel somewhat responsible. How could I have let this affair go on so long? How could I have let her go to him alone to break it off? Between the guilt and grief, I had been eaten alive. Those feelings fueled me in this last month, aided me in the plans that I had created.

I was a shell of myself, which thankfully, made it easy to become someone else.

I have done plenty of things I am not proud of, but everything I have done has been necessary. I am sure of that.

I pull my vehicle into a seemingly abandoned gas station in the middle of nowhere. I park in the familiar spot and get out, sitting down on the curb and staring into a sea of concrete and asphalt. It is not a beautiful sight, but it is somehow very calming. I can see why someone would come here to just exist.

A few semi-trucks are parked in the far back of the lot, their drivers likely sleeping for a few hours before traveling through the night.

A rustling behind me alerts me to movement in the bushes and I see a figure emerge, approaching me wordlessly before sitting down.

"I still can't believe she is alive." He says quietly.

I toss a pebble into the endless asphalt, imagining skipping rocks in the pond as a kid. "I can't either. I thought everything was ruined when Katherine killed Billy so quickly."

"We figured it would take months to convince her, definitely enough time to find Marnie and be away from any suspicion in his murder. I guess it turned out she didn't need much convincing." A deep throaty laugh escapes him.

"Yeah, he deserved it even more than we thought."

"I heard about the other missing women. It was almost Marnie. I can't believe I almost lost a sister…especially so soon after losing Mom."

"Well, we didn't. It all worked out." I fight that familiar rush of emotions every time I think about how close I was to losing my wife forever.

He nods thoughtfully, his dark eyes staring into the vast parking lot, seemingly focused on nothing.

"Where did you get the hemlock so fast anyway? I figured we were going to have to pull some black-market shit for cyanide." I ask, continuing to turn pebbles in my fingertips before I toss them absentmindedly.

"I found it growing in Mom's backyard. Just a few plants, behind the shed."

"Why would Marnie's mom be growing hemlock?"

"I don't think she did, man. Mom hadn't been mobile enough to deal with gardening or cutting the grass in years. Marnie and Nikolas helped her with all the house stuff. I drove her to all her appointments. That's just how we ended up splitting it."

"Why would Marnie be growing hemlock?" My heart begins to race. This is news to me, very unwelcome news.

"Maybe she had the same idea as us." He shrugs, joining me in tossing pebbles.

"Or maybe she had the same idea as Katherine." I whisper.

Epilogue

Marnie

The shock of Max saving me has still not worn off completely. We have been together most of our lives, so I knew that he loves me, but the things he did proved a whole different level of love. Honestly, it was borderline creepy.

When I left the house the morning of my abduction, after Max confronted me about the affair, I stopped by Nikolas' house to drop off the bag of Tupperware containers for his freezer. Ever since our mother died, he basically has only one food group…beer. I feel responsible to make sure he is okay; he is my baby brother after all.

After piling his freezer full for the week, I raced to Billy's second house, where we normally meet. I think back to our conversation, still feeling the sting of the way everything turned out.

"Max knows." I whisper, pulling away from Billy's embrace.

"What are you talking about?" He asks.

"My husband, Max. He confronted me this morning about us. I told him I would break it off with you."

"Are you here to break it off, then?" He asks, his deep husky laugh feeling entirely too nonchalant for my taste.

"No. I love you, I wouldn't leave you."

"Okay, so let's get a quickie in before I have to leave for the office."

"It is time to act on our plan. We have to kill Max. And Katherine. We might as well just do both at the same time."

"We aren't killing Katherine." Whether from his harsh tone, or the sharp words, I feel like I have been cut.

This is what we have planned for so long, he can't go back on it now. I have held on to this plan in my darkest times over the last year. It has given me hope, been a beckoning light.

"What are you talking about? That's been the plan all along. I knew Max would never leave me; I told you it would come to this eventually." I try my best to keep my voice even, not let him see how much this is frustrating me.

"You heard me, Marnie. We are *not* killing Katherine. She is my wife, and that is never going to change." Billy's words are blunt and final.

"So, you have been stringing me along all this time? You never meant to leave her? I'm just some *whore* for you to use and throw away? I thought you loved me!" There is no keeping calm now. My world is crumbling before me and I am powerless to stop it. I want him to hurt as much as I do right now. "I will tell Katherine. She deserves to know."

He had no words of warning. His face never changed from its emotionless façade. He simply grabbed me by the neck, shoving me to the floor so violently, I was convinced my neck would snap.

As his grip tightened, I told myself that this was the end. This is how I will die. At least the last thing I will ever see on this earth, is the man I love more than words could ever describe.

It is funny the way life can be so full circle sometimes. The hemlock I painstakingly cared for over the last year being used to kill Billy is about as ironic as it gets. It was all for him. I would have done anything.

And now, he is dead.

It shouldn't have been him.

I find myself wondering just how much hemlock I have left.

I hear diet coke hides the taste quite well.

About the Author

Fletcher Felix is a thriller and crime fiction author who spends her time hibernating in her country home, most likely with a cat on her lap.

If you enjoyed *Imposter*, please consider leaving a review and following Fletcher's Facebook and Instagram pages to stay updated on future novels!

Check out Fletcher's other novels-

The Faster You Break: Riley Morgen Series Number One (2025)

Riley Morgen Series Number Two (Releasing 2026)

The Spoiler (2025)

www.ingramcontent.com/pod-product-compliance
Lightning Source LLC
LaVergne TN
LVHW090557110826
845146LV00001B/158

* 9 7 9 8 9 9 3 5 4 0 9 1 7 *